THE TROUBLE WITH VAMPIRES

MISTRESS OF MAYHEM 2

TRINA M. LEE

THE TROUBLE WITH VAMPIRES
Copyright 2020 by Trina M. Lee

Published in Canada

Editor
B. Leigh Hogan

Proofreader
Denise Fortowsky

Cover Artist
Marvin Lee Cover Design

Published by
Trina M. Lee

CHAPTER ONE

Tires squealed. We sped through yet another red light to the shrill blare of horns. With no choice but to trust Rayne's driving skills, I held tight to the passenger door handle, watching over my shoulder as the black truck drew closer.

Without hesitation, its driver barreled through the red light after us, causing further commotion accompanied by the shriek of colliding metal. Somehow the federal agent driving the truck avoided the accident they'd caused.

"Getting closer," I warned, keeping an eye on our tail so Rayne could watch the road ahead.

In response to my update he adjusted our speed, accelerating enough to stay several car lengths ahead of our pursuer but not so much that he lost control. Our goal wasn't to ditch the FPA vehicle but to lead them away from their original target. So far so good.

Using a red decoy car that had been supplied for just this purpose, Rayne, Corr, and I had intercepted the Feds on their way to investigate a frantic 911 call: a man acting strangely had lashed out at a gas station clerk, baring fangs. Both the Federal Para-Intelligence Agency and The Circle of the Veil monitored emergency calls for just this reason.

The Circle didn't take kindly to human authorities treading on supernatural territory, meddling in the business of monsters and magic. They also held a dim view of vampires killing in public, which was how I found myself here now, helping to lead the humans away from the werewolf at the gas station while our people went in to grab him before he could do something even more stupid.

There was no guarantee The Circle wouldn't kill him themselves after showing fangs to a human in public, on a security camera to boot. But keeping him out of FPA custody was a priority. Not only did the human agency kill our kind, they also experimented on us. When they got really lucky, they were even able to recruit a few.

"You're not going to make it through that intersection," Corr said, voice awfully calm for someone in the backseat of a car speeding toward a busy intersection. "There's too much traffic."

"Fuck, I know." Rayne slammed a hand on the steering wheel and, instead of continuing toward the intersection, hit the brakes and cut a hard, fast left into a residential area.

Tires protesting, the small sedan struggled to right itself. Rayne slowed until he regained control and then hit the gas again, speeding down the quiet street of slumbering families. I watched the side mirror for any sign of the FPA truck. Had they caught our sudden disappearance?

Yes, yes they had. The truck rounded the corner, skidding off the main road at a dangerous speed.

My fingers tightened almost painfully on the door handle. "They're still on us."

"Good." With a jerk of his head toward the portable GPS on the dash, Rayne continued down another side street at random. "Can you figure out which street will lead us back to our original route?"

Taking a detour hadn't been in the plans. We intended to lead the pursuing vehicle on a goose chase before luring them to where another team would be waiting to back us up. Of course these missions rarely went according to plan. We'd had to roll with the punches before; why should this be any different?

I tapped the GPS screen, zooming out so I could see the surrounding area on the map. "Take a right at the next stop sign. Then your second left. It will take us out another exit from this neighborhood."

"Maybe we should confront them," Corr suggested, gripping the side of my seat. "If we stop here in a neighborhood filled with innocent civilians, they'll have to retreat. They can't very well open fire on us right here."

"That's actually not a bad idea." I glanced at Rayne for his opinion.

Fingers tight on the wheel, his eyes were solid wolf, a deep but vibrant gold. Seeing them like that always made my insides spark with excitement.

"I can't be the first one to stop. If The Circle finds out, they'll have my hide. Literally, I'm sure. Unless they force us to stop, we have to keep moving toward our destination." After taking the next corner with a shriek of burning rubber, Rayne grabbed my hand and kissed the back of it before returning both hands to the wheel.

In the month or so since I'd been forced onto this Mayhem Task Force the two of us had grown close. Too close, some might say. Because close was dangerous. But so was alone. So we deemed our blossoming relationship to be worth the risk.

Rayne wasn't the only one I'd forged a connection with. Some of the people on my team had become friends. A few of them had started to become something more than that. One of those people was my superior, an incubus demon who made my panties drop with just a glance. That attraction promised misfortune, since I hated pretty much everything about him and how he came into my life. The Circle sent Nova to apprehend me for a crime I deemed total bullshit. I hadn't done anything wrong. Killing men who preyed on women would never be wrong. Although I could have chosen a better location.

Nova and I had engaged in one encounter that went farther than it should have. Since then we'd done all we could to avoid close proximity. His incubus touch meant that, every time we got physical, my attraction to him would grow.

Like a craving. An addiction.

Nova had assured me that his craving for me grew as well. I still hadn't decided if I liked that or not. Perhaps the most dangerous part of our fiery desire was how much shit it could get us both in with higher ups should The Circle find out.

With the FPA truck racing along behind us, we sped toward the street that would take us back to the main thoroughfare. The agents had gained some ground but seemed to be keeping their distance. Maybe they worried about drawing citizen attention in the middle of the night?

Right away I had my answer. Up ahead a dark gray SUV shot out in front of us. Parked sideways, it blocked our exit. We had Feds on both sides.

"Son of a bitch." Rayne slammed a palm on the wheel as he hit the brakes, bringing us into a skid. "You guys know the drill. Don't let them take you. Blaze, be ready to drive us out of here."

All I could do was nod as I grabbed my dagger from the floor. The guys had been wolves long enough to know how to shift their skin in a few seconds without flashing innocent bystanders. By the time the Feds had spilled out of their vehicles, I had two large wolves on either side of me, one raven black and the other ashy blond.

Corr faced the truck that screeched to a stop behind us. Rayne faced the newcomers ahead. I stood between the two of them, glancing between each vehicle, trying to assess which team posed the greater threat.

The two men in the tailing truck reached us first. When they opened fire I raised the dagger that Nova had given me, and the blade glowed a soft yellow-gold. The glow spread out to cover us in a protective shield.

As the bullets bounced off the shield to fall harmlessly to the ground, I realized they weren't bullets at all. They were tranquilizer darts. Somehow, that concerned me more than a kill shot. They wanted to take us in.

I glanced back at the second FPA team to find them striding toward us. Three of them. Two women and a man. All human, as the majority of FPA agents tended to be.

"Careful, guys," I said, voice low. "I'm not sure how many of those tranqs it takes to bring any of us down, and I'd rather not find out."

Rayne bumped his furry black head against my leg before turning to bare fangs at the duo as they reloaded. He knew how many it took. He'd been shot with one before. If one dart took down a shifter, a few would do me in too.

Corr didn't wait for the men to take aim again. The ash-blond wolf lunged from my right, tackling an agent to the ground. The guy's gun jerked and went off, the dart nailing his partner in the neck.

Leaving Corr to handle the two of them, Rayne and I prepared to meet the incoming team. Two of them leveled weapons on us. The third, a gray-haired man in the middle, brought his people to a stop well out of reach.

"Call your wolf off," he raised his voice just enough to be heard. So they were concerned about the nearby civilians. "This doesn't have to end bloody."

"Then why do you have guns?" Acting as the voice for the three of us, I held the dagger ready for any shots they might take. Thanks to demon magic, the blade would help protect us. But I knew better than to rely too heavily on any one thing to save me. In the end, I had to save myself.

Corr stood on the chest of the man he'd downed, snarling into his face. The other agent had succumbed to the tranq dart, passed out hard.

"Because we don't have fangs and magic." He shrugged like that should be self-explanatory. "We don't want a scene here any more than you do. Let's just call it a day, shall we?"

"Just like that?" I scoffed. "You expect us to believe that you're going to let us leave peacefully? Then why the hell did your men chase us through the city?"

"Because they thought you were someone else. Just the way you planned it. Am I right?" Hooking a thumb in the waist of his wide pants, the Fed rocked on his heels, waiting for me to make a move.

Opting not to respond to his question, I parried one of my own back at him. "Well, now that you know we're not who you thought we were, why not just leave?"

The man's face split into an ugly grin. "You first. Unless of course you'd prefer that we take you instead."

Rayne's lips peeled back in a snarl and a sinister growl spilled out.

I braced myself and the dagger blade glowed brighter in response. "You can try. I wouldn't recommend it if you want to make it home tonight."

I didn't like to kill, not outside the victims I carefully selected to feed my hunger. But if it was us or them, I wouldn't stop until we were the last ones standing. This guy could make that choice for all of us.

Clenching his thick hands into fists, the Fed's face reddened. Had he expected us to cower and flee? By the way he blubbered and spat, he had. "I'd love to see how much attitude you still have after spending some time in our facility, bitch." With a nod to the women flanking him, he pulled a gun from a holster on his hip. "Dart their asses."

The women held tranq guns, but he held a real one. Shots went off. Using the moves I'd spent hours honing with Nova, I deflected them all. With Corr at our backs and Rayne at my side, I advanced on the three of them, the glowing blade helping me push forward unharmed.

"It's not working." One woman shouted the obvious. "Fall back."

"Not until I say fall back," the man snapped despite the fact that he too walked backward as we advanced.

"We came for one werewolf and that one isn't here." This from the second woman who eyed the narrowing distance to their SUV. "Let's go. This wasn't part of the order."

"So fucking what? They're supes. We can still take them in." Fumbling another clip from his inside pocket, the man never took his eyes off us.

Both women exchanged a look but neither contested the asshole's decision. Their mistake. One I couldn't let stand.

Making the best of their brief dissent, I rushed them. Moving superhumanly fast, I was on them in a blink. With one hand I swept the dagger in an arc, aiming for the man's gun hand. The blade sliced clean through his forearm, and his hand dropped to the ground, still gripping the weapon.

In the few seconds it took the women to react, I threw a telekinetic attack that blasted both against their SUV. If they were smart, they'd flee before they lost any parts.

They seemed to read my mind. Scrambling into the vehicle, they didn't hang around to find out what would happen to the asshole now on his knees and screaming while he clutched his bleeding stump.

I simply couldn't resist.

Dropping my weapon, I was on him. My fangs plunged into his neck, cutting of his wail. Blood filled my mouth, quenching the hunger that I'd spent seven decades learning to master. A hunger that could not be tamed, merely satiated. Until the next time.

I took what I needed before letting him slump to the asphalt in a growing pool of his own blood. Whirling, I found Corr still standing guard over the two agents from the truck. I did a quick survey of nearby houses. Nobody around. No front doors faced us, so no doorbell cams. Hopefully no one had cameras up to catch vandals or teenagers sneaking out.

Grabbing my dagger, I approached the man pinned under Corr. His partner was still out cold. Because I didn't want or need to kill anyone else tonight, I decided to give him the chance I knew his people wouldn't have given me.

"We're going to let you up. You'll grab your friend and leave. Try anything, and you die like your colleague over there." I extended my dagger so the point was mere inches from his face. "Nod if you understand."

The frightened man already lay trapped beneath the burly wolf. Face ashen, he nodded vigorously, willing to take any chance to get out of this alive. Since werewolves could smell a lie, I glanced to Corr for confirmation. The wolf lingered just a second longer before backing off to allow the agent up.

As agreed, the terrified man grabbed his friend and unceremoniously stuffed him into the truck before peeling away with a squeal of tires. The three of us were quick to follow suit.

Once back in the car, I threw it into gear and beat it out of that neighborhood. As far as run-ins with the Feds went, it could have been worse. Only one person had died, and that had been his choice.

Next to me Rayne sat naked and human, dressing in the awkward confines of the passenger seat while Corr did the same in the back. "Head back to where we picked this thing up. As long as we don't run into anyone else, it should be safe to ditch the car and go back to the house." Rayne tugged a black t-shirt over his head, hiding chiseled abs from sight.

Probably for the best. I didn't need the distraction. I glanced in the rearview mirror to check for a tail, but we pulled back onto the busy road without issue.

"Dude pissed himself," Corr said, derision in his usually calm voice. "Haven't scared someone that bad in a while."

I met his gray-hued blue eyes in the mirror. They were a strange shade that could be seen as either color. When their edges crinkled with his smile, a warmth to spread through my chest, helping me relax.

It took several minutes for the tension to leave my body. Although I wasn't opposed to a face-off with the FPA if necessary, it always came with a lot of anxiety. I feared the spilling of my own blood and the wild magic that ran rampant when it happened, taking down anyone in its path whether friend or foe. Thankfully, my magic had not wreaked havoc. This time.

But it would again, as it had before, and I had to be ready when it did.

CHAPTER TWO

Blonde ponytail bouncing, Dalyn spoke animatedly about the excitement her team had endured. She'd accompanied Tavi, Ghost, and Ira to pick up the shifter the Feds had been after. "This other car just came out of nowhere. I thought it was going to T-bone us, but it just caught the fender instead." As she chatted a mile a minute, Dalyn poured a dollop of white wine into a glass with a shaky hand. "There were three agents in that car. I almost shit my pants when one of them stuck a gun in my face, but Ghost came to my rescue." She flashed a dreamy smile at the vampire before slugging back her whole drink in one swallow.

Ghost regarded her with a soft smile that was somehow both sinister and inviting. He tugged the tip of her ponytail in a brotherly fashion on his way out of the kitchen. "Nobody fucks with Sabrina the Teenage Witch on my watch."

Her smile faltered. "Teenage witch? I'm twenty-five, you dick. Although I've been told I can pass for eighteen." Dalyn shook her empty glass at Ghost's retreating back before fetching a refill. She almost collided with Tavi who munched a chicken leg from the fridge in the middle of the kitchen.

"Bullshit you can," Tavi sneered around a mouthful of roasted meat. "And I can pass for a middle-aged white guy."

A few of us had gathered around the island in the kitchen upon returning to Mayhem House. Rayne had gone for a dip in the pool out back while Corr had retreated to his room. I expected Nova to drop in, so I didn't venture far.

My stomach twisted at the thought of seeing him. In the past few weeks Nova and I had kept our hands off each other with increasing difficulty. And yet, I craved that moment when I laid eyes on him and the resulting rush it gave me. The stolen kiss, or the several we'd succumbed to, might have played a role in the way my insides melted into lava every time Nova came around.

The sound of the front door nabbed my attention. Curious, I left Tavi and Dalyn to throw barbs, venturing around the corner into the large entryway.

"Where's Rayne?" Nova barked when he saw me standing there.

Not the nicest of greetings. Able to sense the high-strung energy wrapped tight around him, I bit back the sassy response on the tip of my tongue. "In the pool."

Nova shoved by me toward the large living room that took up most of the main floor's south wing. Before he turned the corner to the hallway, he paused and pointed a finger at me. "Don't go anywhere. I want to see you alone before I leave."

A shiver crept over me, causing my spine to stiffen. Alone? It wasn't often that Nova let himself be alone with me now. Most of our quality time was spent with the rest of the team.

While I waited, I paced around the foyer with growing unease. If anything Nova most likely wanted to touch base about the job tonight, get a play-by-play breakdown, so to speak. So why did I feel so jittery? Already my skin was on fire at the thought of being alone with him.

All this tension and angst because of one encounter that went too far. Who would have thought that one orgasm could change everything? Since the night Nova got me off in the garage, the dynamic between us had been altered. Now I possessed an unnatural draw to him. The worst part was that I'd known the incubus touch was addictive, and I'd welcomed it anyway.

Even now, when I let my mind go back to that night, I still wondered how much better it would feel to have all of him.

Perhaps the most ridiculous part of it all was that Nova and I weren't particularly fond of one another. We weren't vicious enemies, but the animosity between us only seemed to fuel our attraction.

Nova had a tendency to go harder on me than the others. He liked to push me until my temper flared, until I was ready to tear him apart. He wasn't all bad though. Despite the whole demon thing, he had a sliver of goodness hidden inside that black heart. I saw it the night he offered me freedom, despite what it would cost him to help me run from The Circle of the Veil.

Choosing to stay had just felt right. Running wouldn't prove anything, just keep me firmly entrenched as a victim, like my sire had once made me. But that wasn't me anymore. And I was here to prove it.

"How did everything go tonight, cherry bomb?"

Nova's sensual voice startled me out of my thoughts. I turned from the painting I'd been absently staring at to find him leaning against the wall, arms crossed. He kept his distance yet made no effort to keep from drinking in the sight of me.

Keenly aware of the way that crimson gaze ate up every inch of my body, I tried not to squirm under its weight. "We killed one of theirs. But really, it could have gone worse."

Listening attentively as I recapped the events of our outing, Nova nodded as I spoke. Jet-black hair fell past his shoulders with several braids tied into it including three rows tight to one side of his head. A tiny black feather hung from the end of one.

Over the several weeks that I'd known him, I'd grown accustomed to Nova's appearance, his true visage: the way his horns curled up off his head, the gentle swish as his snake-like tail drifted lazily about behind him.

As I spoke, I took my chance to eat up the eye candy too. Dressed in black pants and a sleeveless hooded tunic, large wings hugging his back, Nova looked good enough to eat. Would that really be a problem?

He snapped fingers in front of my face.

I jerked back with a gasp. "What the hell are you doing?"

"You've got that look in your eyes again," Nova teased, wagging a scolding finger in my face. "Careful now, Blaze. One of these nights my will is going to fail me. Might want to work on yours." Despite the teasing lilt to his words, he remained stiff.

Unable to resist with him so close, I darted my tongue out to lick the tip of that finger. "What's with you tonight, Nova?" I asked, gliding my thumb over the back of his hand. "You seem wound up. Did something happen?"

"Not yet, and I'd like to keep it that way." He glanced around the foyer before ushering me into the small sitting room off the entryway. He steered me over to the couch under the window, but neither of us sat down. "The Feds sent people after both of our teams. They're keeping tabs on you all now."

"Well, yeah, of course they are. Wouldn't you if you were them?" As the intensity of Nova's closeness grew, I crossed my arms, hugging myself in an attempt to keep from touching him further.

"Yeah, I would." Rubbing the faint trace of stubble along his jaw, Nova gazed out the window at the dark driveway. "That's what bothers me. I have to send some of you in, to get closer to them."

"And that's a problem because?" Try as I might to stomp it down, Nova was making me nervous.

When he paused, staring out into nothing, that feeling grew. Finally he swung his intense gaze my way. "Because I'm not sure you're ready for what you'll be asked to do. I don't want your blood magic to make you a liability when it should make you the greatest asset here."

Nova had far more faith in my abilities than I did. My magic was wild, erratic. It refused to follow direction and rampaged like a rabid animal. But it wasn't going anywhere. I'd lived this way for long enough to know that much at least.

Weaving my fingers together, I clasped my hands tight, doing all I could not to reach for him. Goddamn that incubus pull. "Then help me prepare for whatever it is The Circle will want," I said, trying not to call him out and failing. "You promised to help with my blood magic, but you can't stand to be alone with me long enough to get anywhere."

"I'm alone with you right now, and all I can think about is peeling your clothes off with my teeth." With a sexy half grin, Nova nodded to the couch. "Laying you on that couch. Fucking you until this constant craving is finally satisfied. For a while."

My breath came faster as the room warmed with his erotic charge. "Maybe if you did, we'd finally be able to get some work done on my magic without all of this tension getting in the way."

That gorgeous smile turned into a tangible laugh, one I could almost wrap around me like a velvet cloak. "You're too daring for your own good, firecracker. Careful what you wish for; you just might get it. And I can't be held responsible for what happens after. Not if you keep asking for it."

Nova wasn't wrong. I had asked for it a few times now, literally. He hadn't given in. When the rush of being around him wore off, I'd been glad for his resistance. I couldn't imagine I'd make it long in this house if we gave in to our urges. If the yearning was this bad now, I probably didn't want to discover how much worse it could get.

"I know, but none of that will even be a problem once I'm dead. Bottom line." There was no point pretending this situation wasn't a death sentence. We survived on a nightly basis around here.

The predatory glint in his eyes softened though the sex-charged hunger remained. He tipped his head in acknowledgement of defeat. "Fine. Let's go to the basement."

CHAPTER THREE

The air smelled of incense and burnt sulfur. As Nova led me into the magic wing of the basement for the first time, I rubbed the goosebumps that prickled on my skin. Magic hung heavy on the atmosphere.

I wasn't sure what I expected at the end of the long hall, but it wasn't an elaborate old library complete with a spiral staircase that led up to a reading loft. Pausing just inside the threshold, I took it all in. Deep, rich wood tones made up the book-laden shelves as well as the desk in one corner. A fire burned in a hearth surrounded by fluffy easy chairs. Most of the large library was just that: walls lined with books and a place to study them.

An arched doorway on the other side opened into a wide-open space lit by dozens of candles in sconces. A pentagram inside a circle painted in white shone against the black floor. That's where the awful vibes drifted from. Magic came from many places, and the darker, the deadlier. The room felt stuffed with several energy types. I couldn't pick the magic in the air apart the way some vampires and demons could.

Nova didn't seem bothered by it, like he barely noticed. "This room is safe for magic, especially if performed inside the circle. If your magic goes wild in here, it can only harm who and what is in this room with you."

"All right." Cracking my knuckles, I sucked in a deep breath. "Are you going to teach me symbol magic?"

"Not yet. First, there's something you really need to work on." Steepling his fingers, Nova turned his usual bossy expression on me, the one that meant he was about to push me out of my comfort zone.

"And what might that be?" A hard edge crept into my tone. Nova's tendency to go hard on me, especially when he was in a mood, worked my nerves like nothing else.

"Magical control comes second. First you need to learn to control your mind." Tapping a fingertip against his temple, Nova ambled to the fire. With a poker from the stand next to the hearth, he prodded the logs.

The firelight glinted off his face, highlighting the sharp angles of his jaw. Every detail appeared to be perfectly planned and executed. He was a work of art. Each time I got a chance to really observe him, I found something new and wonderful about him. Not that I'd ever say so out loud.

"Yeah, I have some issues. I'm aware." Averting my gaze when he glanced up to find me staring, I touched a book on the nearest shelf at random. Nope, not gawking at the sexy incubus demon. Not at all.

"At some point they will get their hands on you, Blaze. I want you to be ready when they do." Replacing the poker, Nova extended a hand toward the circle through the archway. "We'll take it slow. But we have to start somewhere."

Something about the way he said that made me want to go pretty much anywhere other than through that doorway. "Do we though? I think learning hands on during FPA encounters has been going well so far."

Nova's mocking laughter rang throughout the vast library. "Your denial is adorable but ultimately useless. Not to mention, total bullshit."

Despite my feigned interest in the books on the shelves, Nova ushered me along toward the magical circle. Using a big black wing, he kept me moving, even when I resisted under the archway.

"What are you so afraid of, cherry bomb? Me? Or yourself?"

Those words ignited my pride, and I shoved away from him, striding into the middle of the pentagram. It felt as if the tendrils of residual magic stuck to me like the fragments of a broken spiderweb. Rubbing my arms briskly did nothing to remove the sensation.

"You'd love that, wouldn't you? If I said you scared me." Standing in the middle of the large pentagram, I shot him a smirk. "Does my fear mean that much to your ego?"

"Of course not. I'm an incubus." Sauntering toward me with extra swagger in his step, Nova held up a palm. A small ice shard hovered in the center. "I'd much rather you desire me than fear me. Although I can work with either."

"Right. So what do you plan to do with that?" Wary, I eyed the sharp sliver of ice.

Nova's blood-red eyes gleamed with wicked amusement. "We can't very well work on your blood magic unless you bleed."

My defensive instincts rose up, ready to fight. The closer each step brought him, the more I bristled. No part of me wanted to do this, but this practice was no longer optional. If The Circle ever discovered how easily my blood magic could blow an operation, they'd wipe me out as a risk.

"Fair enough," I muttered, my mouth suddenly dry.

The walls surrounding the circle were bare and beige: No breakables to fall and smash. Nothing in here but the circle on the floor and the candles in their sconces, which appeared to be securely affixed to the wall. And no way out other than through the archway from the library, which Nova conveniently blocked.

As soon as he stepped into the ritual circle with me, the atmosphere responded by warming with sensual energy. The lust might have caused me to let my guard down if he hadn't whipped that ice shard. It whistled as it flew past my ear, shattering against the wall behind me. A second and third followed fast, forcing me to move quick to avoid being slashed.

"Is this really the best way to test my magic?" I snapped, irritated by his come-at-me approach. "Is the attack aspect really necessary? Why not just cut me?"

"The Feds won't just walk up and give you a little paper cut. They'll throw what they have at you, and you will bleed. Just like you did before." For good measure, Nova followed up with one more shard, three times larger than the others. Now he was just being a dick.

Temper flaring, I flung out both hands and hit him with a shot of telekinetic power. It plowed into his chest, shoving him back with a stumble. The demon just laughed and raised both hands to invite more. Gritting my teeth, I flung a second shot, annoyed when he blocked it. I didn't have the power he did. The only way I stood a chance against him was using my blood magic, and we both knew it.

I faltered, dropping my hands. "Come on, Nova. Do we really have to do this whole song and dance?"

Before I could continue my protests, Nova darted forward, more a blur than actual motion. He caught hold of me and spun me around in his arms, pressing my back to his chest. Grabbing both of my wrists in one of his, he pinned me tight.

Brushing a lock of hair off my cheek, Nova's breath tickled my ear. "You know we do. How else will you know how to react when someone has you trapped?"

Trapped. That word alone made my insides quiver with discomfort. Though I wanted to believe Nova had my best interests in mind, the feeling of being unable to break free from him triggered the panic that Remington had cultivated in me.

"Stop." Breathy, my voice was barely there. Nova was nothing like Rem. Still I froze in the grip of memories that threatened to overtake me. Just being held like this triggered my response to fight like hell.

"Let yourself feel it." Nova's gentle murmur soothed while his vice-like hold provoked. "The anger. The fear. All of it. Do you feel how powerful it is?"

Frantically I shook my head, tossing red tendrils in my face. "I don't want to do this."

Nova tightened his grip until my wrists ached, crushed together in his grasp. He jerked me hard against him, making my teeth clack together. "You don't have a choice. The FPA won't give you a choice either. You can't allow your emotions to run away with you. Control them and you control the magic."

Chest heaving, I struggled against him, testing his solid hold. I couldn't overpower a demon. Certainly not this demon.

He made it sound so easy. Nothing about my magic had ever been easy. "Don't you think I've tried that?" I snapped, straining against him. "It's not that simple."

"Nothing worth doing well is ever easy." Another ice shard appeared in Nova's free hand. He held it ready, letting me get a good look at the sharp edges. "You don't belong to him anymore, Blaze. You never really did."

I heard the powerful truth in his words. It resonated like an echo within me. So fucking badly I wanted to embrace it, to let it fuel my reaction. But when Nova brought that icy blade down, dragging it across my forearm, I lost control.

The cut wasn't that deep. Just enough to let the blood spill, and with it, the power rose. Like an expanding bubble it filled me, seeking and finding the outlet it needed. It burst out, limited by the tiny amount of blood that flowed. Still, it gave me enough strength to break free of Nova.

Throwing my hands wide, I flung him off like an old garment. When the first drop of blood splashed against the floor, the pentagram glowed the soft red of my aura.

I whirled on Nova who stood his ground in the face of my volcanic magic. He opened his mouth to speak, and the next moment he'd been pasted against the wall, wings splayed on either side of him, his feet well above the floor. I didn't mean for it to nail him like that.

A cough racked him, and he sucked in a harsh breath, which turned into a bark of laughter. "You really have to work on holding back for the right moment. It's impossible to instruct you when you won't wait for instruction."

Fists clenched tight at my sides, I fumed that the demon had enough audacity to laugh. Didn't he see that I was scared shitless here? "It's impossible to learn from someone who won't listen when I tell them that I can't fucking control this shit." My shout drove a second shot of wild magic, weaker than the first as my wound's flow slowed.

Ready for it, Nova raised a hand to deflect the blast down into the center of the pentagram behind me. The light surrounding it glowed brighter as the core of the circle absorbed the power. Then the light dimmed and went out.

"The magic absorbed by the circle feeds the wards that protect the house and property," he explained even though I hadn't asked.

When I stood there staring at him with teeth and fists clenched, his wings lifted and resettled against him. Those wings often revealed his true thoughts, even when no other part of him did. He had to school himself to remain neutral at this distance from me, though I couldn't discern more from that single shift.

When several moments passed and neither of us spoke, I decided that I'd had enough. I stormed from the circle, aware Nova wouldn't let me walk out on him. Not when I had to pass right by him to reach the exit.

As anticipated, he stepped into my path, but he made no other effort to trap me. "I'm trying to help you, dammit. I've never seen any vampire do what you can do. Only the panic cripples your control. If you can master your emotions, you'll master your magic."

I'd never known the blood magic without panic guiding its force. Its mere existence terrified me. Since the first time it had exploded out like dynamite going off in my hands, I had feared it.

Remington had possessed blood magic as well. Supernatural power tended to be passed among a vampire's bloodline, manifesting to various degrees in all those they sired. However, his blood magic hadn't been driven by panic and fear. He could slice his palm to amplify his power with the blood while standing there calm and smiling the entire time.

Not me though.

Of course, I hadn't done much smiling during my time with Rem. He'd brought me screaming into this underworld. The sick affection he'd bestowed on me made sense only to him, and he always followed up with more abuse and pain. While ruminating on his abuse, the night Remington turned me threatened to flash through my memory.

I shoved Nova in an effort to flee both him and my past.

He caught me gently by the upper arms and peered down into my wide, frantic eyes. "I am not him. Despite the circumstances, you're safe here, safe with me. I'm going to help you, Blaze. Please trust me."

A calm settled over me, over everything. I knew he created it, but I didn't care. I leaned into Nova, letting the coziness of his gentle vibes lull me back down to the here and now.

Placing a hand on his chest, I felt the steady, strong beat of his heart beneath my palm. I couldn't help but wish I could find what I needed in Nova. But we couldn't be together, and I wasn't sure I even knew what I sought.

Holding his studious gaze, I let myself fall into the seductive pull of being so close to him. Touching him. Just for a moment. Up on my tiptoes, I kissed him, deep and yearning. A silent cry in the dark. A plea for so much more than he could give me. An apology for what I could not give him: trust.

Faith that I was safe with him.

Nova didn't deserve to be punished for someone else's crimes. Nobody deserved to pay the price for what Remington had done to me.

Right before I broke away, I whispered against Nova's lips, "You have no idea how much I wish I could do that."

CHAPTER FOUR

Do you want me to be there next time? You don't have to do this alone." Rayne traced the outline of the small gash from Nova's ice shard, which sent a ticklish jolt skipping up my arm, teasing my nerve endings. "Maybe Nova isn't the right one to teach you."

The steady thud of his heart against me both soothed and stimulated. I let my head fall against his shoulder. Hot water and bubbles covered all but our shoulders and heads. It felt amazing.

Between his legs, his chest to my back, I could feel the slight swell of his semi-erect cock. Dragging my fingertips through the bubbly water, I watched it swirl and separate beneath my touch.

"If Nova doesn't teach me, nobody ever will. Rem never would, but I don't think he understood my magic either. I don't know anyone else who can help. The problem isn't Nova anyway. It's me." It wasn't a self-pitying statement. Just truth. A truth I was determined to change.

Since Nova had let me walk out of the library, leaving him behind, I'd replayed our final moments together. Several times. Surely Nova knew how his plea had sounded. Trust a demon? Was anyone foolish enough to fall for that? The number of people I'd trusted in my life had been non-existent until recently. People for the most part, whether human or other, were scum. Plain and simple.

Not the werewolf using a sudsy bath puff to drizzle bubbles down over the two of us. Rayne had proven himself to give a damn about others, to the point of putting himself at risk. A wolf's loyalty ran far and deep, but it was not easily given.

I didn't take that confidence lightly.

We'd formed a flirtatious friendship from the start, much to my surprise. He was easy going, fun to talk to, and a partner who really had my back. And for the first time in pretty much my entire existence, I felt genuine affection for a man.

It hadn't been forced on me like the Stockholm Syndrome I'd spent decades recovering from, nor had it been obligatory like the naïve love I'd had for my father before he bargained me away. It was authentic, and it scared the shit out of me.

I told Rayne that I wasn't looking for love. Since Nova liked to remind us that we shouldn't get attached to one another in this house, I was wary of feeling too much. Falling too deep. I'd spent far too many years mourning a love I'd never known, longing for the deep emotion that the world promised was worth dying for.

Now I stood on the precipice of trust, asking myself if I should take the leap, and then Nova had the goddamn nerve to ask me to trust him of all people. Not just ask but plead. For something I couldn't give him. Not now. Not yet. Maybe not ever.

"Nova goes too hard on you though." Rayne pulled me from my thoughts. "He's a button pusher that doesn't always know when to stop."

"Doesn't know? Or doesn't care?" I smirked to myself, cupping a handful of bubbles.

"Both, although Nova has taken a liking to you. For some reason, it makes him more of an asshole than usual." The laugh that shook Rayne's chest lacked mirth. Reaching around from behind, he pulled my hand closer and blew the bubbles from my palm up into the air above us.

They danced overhead, breaking apart, darting in several directions as the tiny air currents in the room caught them. One small bubble floated down to settle on the tip of my nose, and I laughed it out of existence.

Some might have mistaken Rayne's annoyance for jealousy. I knew that it wasn't. Rayne had made his interest in me clear. However, he also knew that we were on borrowed time. Rather than carving out the details of a relationship forged under shitty circumstances, we'd opted to just enjoy one another. One night at a time.

I didn't hide anything from Rayne. Not the one night stand I'd had with Ghost prior to coming to Mayhem House nor the encounter I'd shared with Nova after. For the most part, Rayne was cool with it. Cool enough to share an encounter with Ghost and me, before Nova had rudely interrupted, ending it before it could really start.

"He knows how to work my temper, that's for sure. Sometimes it helps. Rage sure beats panic." A tendril of hair had escaped my bun, and I blew it out of my eyes. The sun had risen a while ago. I was almost ready to move to the bed for some much-needed slumber. "So tell me about the new guy. Trouble already? Is that what Nova was in a mood about?" If Nova had to track the new guy down, he was a goner by now.

In the five weeks or so that I'd been at Mayhem House, several new recruits had come and gone. Some had run, taking their chances, while others had chosen death over joining our Mayhem Task Force.

Our number remained unchanged.

"Yeah. Not much to tell. Sent him out with Corr, and he took off. Nova tracked him down. I didn't expect him to last long." Rayne's hands dipped beneath the water to glide over my wet body.

"You didn't expect me to last this long either," I pointed out. As he caressed my sides, triggering a ticklish spot, a playful laugh escaped me.

Rayne lightly teased my nipples into matching taut points before continuing his underwater exploration of my body. "Hey, I didn't expect myself to still be here now. I guess anything can happen." He said that last bit in a manner that suggested he meant something else. Something more.

Beneath the layer of bubbles covering the water's surface, Rayne's hand slid over my stomach and down between my legs. The immediate sensation of the sudden touch made me suck in a breath. With the faintest touch he dragged a fingertip over my clit, a tease before moving away to stroke along my slit.

It didn't take much to turn me on right now. Every time I was around Nova, I left feeling like I needed half-a-dozen orgasms to rid me of the sexual tension. Rayne often served as the recipient of those urges, not that he minded.

I moaned softly as he kept up the teasing touches. Behind me his cock grew harder, making some demands of its own. That was fair.

Reaching up to run a wet hand along the side of his face, I said, "Is it just me, or is the water starting to get cold?"

"In other words, you want to get out and fuck now." Rayne laughed, dragging his finger around my clit in lazy circles, never quite touching.

"What can I say? You can read me like a book." Turning over so we were face to face, I wrapped a hand around the rock-hard shaft straining between us. "If I'm not mistaken, part of you wants to get out and fuck too." I wiggled both brows at him, grinning when he gave a melodramatic groan.

"Nope, not mistaken," he confirmed. "Many parts of me want to pin you to the bed right now."

"Then what are we waiting for?"

If it had been a race to see who could get out and get dried faster, I'd have lost. Not that I wasn't eager to get into bed. Once Rayne was standing on the bathmat, dripping water while rubbing a towel over his damp hair, I took my time, enjoying the sight of him.

"Better hurry your ass up, Blaze. Last one to the bed is the first one to give oral." To top off his challenge, Rayne whipped my bare ass with his wet towel before darting to the bed. He made it in two lengthy strides.

"Your challenges get more ridiculous each time." Standing in view of the bed from the bathroom, I slowly toweled off, taking my sweet time. Rayne's golden eyes followed my every move.

"You love them."

I did. Rayne could be a total goofball, and it was adorable as fuck.

As I made my way to him, I found a number of reasons to stop along the way. Noticing a scuff mark on the floor, asking about the fisherman painting that hung above the fireplace, whatever it took to drive him a little nuts.

Sprawled out in the middle of the bed, blankets fluffed up all around him, Rayne crossed his arms behind his head and watched me with predatory wolf eyes. "You're going to make me smack that gorgeous ass of yours, aren't you?"

In response I paused to shake my booty at him before crawling onto the foot of the bed. "It's all yours, baby."

"Remember you said that." A growl edged his warning. The weight of his beastly stare caused my core to tighten.

Following the rules of Rayne's made-up-on-the-spot challenge, I grasped his thick shaft and sucked the head of his cock into my mouth.

The rumble of Rayne's growl intensified. He plunged a hand into my hair, tugging and twisting as he worked my bun loose. "Sorry," he murmured when he inadvertently pulled too hard. Once my long red locks were free, he tousled my hair so it fell about my shoulders. "Much better. I like having something to hold onto."

I'd noticed. Rayne could be a real hair puller at times, which never detracted from our engagements. As I gave him my best oral affection, his grip on my locks tightened until he pulled me off. Even though I was happy to make him come, he wanted more than my mouth.

Seizing hold of one wrist, Rayne used it to tug me closer. Staying in his relaxed position on his back, he patted his lap with a wink. Needing no further coaxing, I straddled his hips.

Making a show of his lazy approach, Rayne laid back and let me guide his cock between my legs. So I teased the hell out of him by slipping just the head inside me before pulling back.

That's when Rayne gave me a resounding smack on one ass cheek. Four wolf fangs protruded from beneath his lips when he spoke. "If you make me come before I even get inside you, it will be a week of climactic tease for you."

The sharp sting on my flesh gave way to a warm pleasurable burn. Having him right where I wanted him, I slid down the full length of his shaft with a moan. Rayne's cock stretched me wide as he thrust up into me, burying deep.

"Is that supposed to be a punishment, Rayne? Because it sounds like fun to me." I rolled my hips, taunting as I slid down his length, grinning when it coaxed a husky groan from him.

Being with Rayne allowed me a sense of liberation I'd never had. Taking mostly humans as lovers throughout the years, I hadn't been free to be my full self. Not like I was now, here with him. I doubted that Rayne would ever know the full extent of what he represented in my life: my turning point onto a better path.

"You won't be saying that when it happens." When Rayne tired of the shared effort, he rolled us over. Once I was beneath him, he railed me like the world was ending and this was our last chance at bliss before it all turned to dust.

With his face buried in my scarlet tresses, Rayne kissed my neck, hungry and demanding. His breath came hot and fast next to my ear. The passion with which he took me never ceased to leave me in a state of wonder. So deep was Rayne's affection, it both frightened and fascinated me.

After achieving a mutually satisfying conclusion, he pulled me into his arms and tucked in tight against me. Nuzzling the side of my face in a wolf-like gesture I'd come to know and love, he quickly fell into a soft-snoring slumber with his head next to mine.

I snuggled into his hotblooded warmth. Rayne's bed had become one of my favorite places in the house, a safe haven of sorts.

However, as I lay there in his comforting embrace awaiting the so-called sandman, I couldn't tame my thoughts. They kept taking me back to the library downstairs. To Nova's uncharacteristic plea.

Everybody with half a brain in their head knew better than to trust a demon. Any demon. Evil and deception came with the territory. Literally.

I didn't even know how to trust anyone. I was learning how to do that now. In small steps.

The problem that kept me awake was, despite having every reason why I shouldn't, I wanted to trust Nova. Desperately.

CHAPTER FIVE

I s this really necessary?" Tavi's tone was harsh and critical. With arms crossed she watched Dalyn and me with open judgment. "I can't believe you're letting Nova pimp you like street trash."

Squeezed onto the bench seat with Dalyn in front of the vanity mirror in her room, I carefully smudged the liner around my eyes for a sultry, smoky effect. "He's not pimping us, Tavi. We volunteered. And considering we're little more than prisoners here, the fact that he asked instead of ordered says something."

"Yeah, it says you're fucking him." From behind us Tavi lounged on the bed, running her mouth, dishing the attitude hard. The full moon was right around the corner, and the werewolves in the house were feeling it. Tavi had been more snark-ass than usual.

I couldn't help but laugh. Not only had I gotten used to the bitchy werewolf's candid insults, I'd grown to enjoy them. Because I knew deep down there was a lot more going on with Tavi. Something she didn't seem to know how to deal with. I'd been there, was still there. So I didn't take it personally. Not even when she made it personal.

Turning around on the bench, I fixed her with a calm, focused stare. "I have not fucked Nova. If I was lying, you'd know. So let that one go for a while, would you?"

The werewolf's keen senses made it easy for her to sniff out a lie. I admittedly didn't know how it worked, but it did. Satisfied that she wouldn't catch me in a lie, not today anyway, I spun back around to continue my makeup application.

"Besides, we're not posing as street trash," Dalyn interjected, digging through her cosmetics bag for a lipstick. "We're going as courtesans. High class escorts. The kind that secret agents hire for bachelor parties, not the kind offering ten-dollar blowjobs behind a crack den."

Tavi eyed the blonde witch with scrutiny. "Yeah, and what happens when some sloppy Fed puts their hands all over you? Or wants to stick it to you in the bathroom? Are you willing to do that for the sake of getting information? Personally, I'd rather be dead."

The watchdog team had received intel indicating that several FPA members would be attending a private party tonight. A bachelor party for a colleague, it featured a private penthouse suite with high security. Nobody was getting in who wasn't on the guest list.

Naturally The Circle of the Veil saw potential in a party of drunk federal agents thinking they were safe. There would no doubt be shop talk.

"No one is getting screwed by a drunk Fed in the bathroom." I exchanged a glance with Dalyn beside me, and she smiled, rolling her eyes. "We go in, get what we can, and get out."

"Easy peasy," Dalyn murmured as she carefully daubed a mascara wand along her lower lashes.

Tavi scoffed, shoving the pillows on the bed about until she'd created a nest of them to sprawl across. "Come on, Blaze. You're not that naïve. And if shit goes south? What then?"

"Ghost and Rayne won't be far. It's not like we're going without a backup team. If all goes as planned, they won't even know we're anything other than escorts." After borrowing Dalyn's lipstick, a tone as red as my hair, I checked out my image in the mirror. Definitely not my usual soft wing liner and little else. This look screamed sex kitten. It unnerved me.

"Make sure to push those titties up." Tavi chuckled, a friendly sound that had started to come out more often when the three of us spent time together. "If it's all they can see, maybe they won't notice the fangs."

Snatching a stray pillow from the foot of the bed, I smacked her over the head with it. "They won't see the fangs. I'll be using a glamour."

Nova had promised to provide me with a locket that would house a demon spell. The glamour would make me appear as human as Dalyn who would also be using a mild glamour of her own creation to alter her hair and eye color.

Dressed in a slinky black cocktail dress with a plunging neckline and a slit up one side, I descended the stairs to the main floor, fussing with a stray curl that wouldn't obey. Finally stuffing it behind an ear, I arranged my loose locks so they covered most of my cleavage. No point showing off all the goods until absolutely necessary.

Tavi followed behind Dalyn and me, brow set in a hard frown. When Nova approached us about this, she'd been the first to shoot him down, to no one's surprise. The unfortunate reality was that the FPA had more people than we did. They brought them in from all over the world, some special agents born and bred for their jobs. Though the number of supernatural beings in the city was likely much higher than even the FPA knew, the size of our team didn't compare. And most supes weren't exactly lining up to be part of this task force.

Only the rebels and rule breakers were lucky enough to join our squad, and since a stupid supe was usually a dead supe, there just weren't as many as needed to even the playing field. So if going into this party tonight could get us anything that might help us stay a step ahead, I was willing to take one for the team by pretending to be an escort for a Fed party.

Nova stepped out of the kitchen, laughing at something Retta had said. The resident witchy instructor hadn't approved of us taking on this job either. She'd shaken a finger at Nova and given him a glare that had spoken loud and clear. Much to my shock, the demon had accepted her silent scolding with a don't-kill-the-messenger shrug.

As soon as his crimson gaze landed on me, Nova stopped dead in his tracks. His wings flared behind him, resettling against his back once he pushed forward into motion, recovering from whatever had momentarily tripped him up. The sudden smolder of desire in his gaze gave me an idea of what that might be.

"This is a terrible, terrible idea," he blurted, blatantly ogling me. Realizing how obvious he was, Nova dialed it back. Averting his gaze, he glanced at Dalyn. "Are you sure you're both up to this?"

"Look, Nova," I said, secretly pleased with his reaction, "we all know The Circle isn't giving us the option to say no. If we hadn't volunteered someone would be forced to go regardless. It's easier this way."

On the stairs Tavi had draped herself over the banister, muttering expletives about misogynistic bullshit. With her side shave fresh and the rest of her long black hair falling down to hide one eye, she appeared even more the predator than usual. I envied her ability to always look like someone you wouldn't want to fuck with.

Nova snarled in her direction, baring two large fangs on both the top and bottom. I didn't know if every demon had beastly traits, but it was something I found undeniably sexy about him. Maybe that was just the incubus addiction talking.

From the pocket of his pants he pulled a small gold locket shaped like a star. "Inside this locket is the glamour spell I whipped up. It's made with a potent elixir from the other side. So whatever you do, don't open it. Anyone in close proximity will be hit with a massive hallucinatory effect, you included."

A simple glamour like the one Dalyn used to alter her appearance wasn't enough for me. If for any reason they had some kind of thermal scanner present, they'd read me as a vampire no matter how I looked. Demon magic went beyond the human tech abilities. If Nova's locket told it I was human, that's how it would see me.

"That's not alarming at all." My sarcasm was delivered with a smile that went unappreciated by Nova.

Twirling a finger for me to turn around, Nova stepped up behind me and swept my hair aside. A subtle tremor racked me as he fastened the chain's clasp. He was close enough for me to feel the heat emanating from his hard body. If Dalyn and Tavi hadn't been present, I might have given in to the urge to press my ass against him.

The locket lay against my chest, pretty and inconspicuous. Immediately the locks that tumbled over my shoulders appeared blonde instead of red. Nova turned me around by the shoulders, giving me a scrutinous onceover. "I like you better as a redhead."

I turned toward the mirror above the decorative table and its ever-changing flower display. My reflection still resembled me but different. I saw no fangs in my reflection even though I could feel them with my tongue. Creamy blonde hair and green eyes along with a beauty mark I didn't usually have changed me enough that any Fed who may have seen my red hair in the dark shouldn't easily recognize me. My heavier than usual makeup helped with the disguise as well.

When we stood on the front lawn waiting for the car that would take us to the ritzy hotel where the party would be held, Nova waited with us. I could tell there was something he wanted to say. I also knew that The Circle had given him a job tonight too. Something to do with the black magic wares he bought and sold. All he'd said when prodded was that he was being sent to retrieve something The Circle needed from a demon.

Another reminder of how far apart Nova and I were. We didn't live in the same world. Even though our worlds intersected, he had never been human. He walked on this side and the other, the spirit realm where demons dwelled. I couldn't even imagine what that was like.

When a black car rolled down the driveway, Nova pulled me aside while Dalyn got in. "The Circle might expect you to do whatever it takes to pry some information from those human scum, but I don't. Go as far as you're willing and not an inch further. Because honestly, the thought of any of those assholes laying a finger on you makes me want to go there and burn the entire hotel down before you arrive."

Too quickly he dropped the hand that touched my arm, leaving me wanting for more. The heat that uncoiled within me at his possessive tone caught me off guard. I didn't belong to Nova. Not even close. Still, it felt good that he wanted me to. The fact that it felt good scared me into stepping toward the car.

The demon got inside my head far too easily. We barely liked each other. Lust didn't equal affection and certainly not a relationship.

Because I couldn't leave on such a serious note, I fanned myself like a blushing schoolgirl, not that I'd ever been one. "I am ever so flattered by your concern, dear sir. But I think us women folk can handle ourselves among these lowly human men."

Nova's frown broke, and a smile tugged at his full lips. "I really ought to bend you over and smack that tight ass."

Slipping him an impish grin, I clutched my handbag containing my phone and pursed my red lips. "I'm afraid I'm all booked up this evening. But if you'd like me to work that into my schedule, I'm sure that can be arranged." I flounced to the car and slipped inside, winking at Nova before closing the door.

He watched the car pull away without so much as a muscle twitch. But there was no missing the unspoken promise that lurked in his eyes.

"How can you stand it?" Dalyn asked, glancing back at the demon. "Being around Nova, especially if you're not doing him. Just looking at him too long makes my panties wet."

Covering my mouth to muffle my laughter, I nodded. "Trust me, I know the feeling. He doesn't make it easy, that's for sure."

"He's totally hungry for you." She nudged me with an elbow. "How do you resist? I can't imagine he'd say no if you wanted it."

I couldn't be sure about that. Nova had done an exceptional job of keeping his hands out of my pants since the one and only time. Not that I felt comfortable sharing that with Dalyn. We'd forged a friendship, but we hadn't quite reached that level of intimacy.

"Nova is an incubus," I said as if that explained everything about the demon. "He's probably hungry for anything with a vagina."

If the driver, the same werewolf who'd driven me to my apartment for my things, paid attention to our conversation, he didn't show it. He didn't acknowledge us until we pulled up in front of the hotel, a five-star place overlooking the river. It tended to be the hotel of choice for celebrities and rich executives.

The werewolf, Sage if I recalled correctly, opened the door for us as we exited the car. With a nod and a stiff, forced smile, he was off.

Turning to Dalyn, I ran fingers through my now blonde hair. "Ready? Remember, try not to let anyone take you too far away from me. Stay within earshot if possible. If we get split up and you think your cover might be blown, get out. Using any means necessary."

"I'm not leaving you behind," she said beneath her breath as we passed through the lobby, nodding to the doorman on the way.

"Don't worry about me. You're the fragile human." My tease landed flat, so I cracked a smile to ease the nerves that were settling over each of us. It didn't help much.

Dalyn's expression grew pinched as we strode toward the bank of elevators. A few people lingered in the lobby: a couple checking in, a security guard watching the front door. Nobody glanced twice at us. Hopefully the agents upstairs would be as easy to fool.

"Seriously, Blaze," she said when we were closed inside the small lift. "Survival first. That goes for you too. But we came together and we leave together. I'm not running without you, and I know you wouldn't leave my fragile human ass behind."

Now a hint of amusement lit up her face. Even as a brunette dressed like a mafia queen, she had that bubblegum pop princess vibe. It was adorable. The tight red minidress she wore hugged her hourglass curves. She'd have no trouble getting some shithead's attention.

"Fine, whatever you say, Karen," I quipped with a giggle. We'd been instructed to use fake names. I already technically did, but I had an arsenal of them.

"Fuck you," she hissed with a bark of laughter. "If I'm Karen then you're Cheryl."

"But I've never had a she-shed." My mock disappointment was met with more laughter. Nervous laughter. The numbers above the elevator door ticked higher, feeding our jitters. Only the fanciest of suites graced the top floor. The Feds spared no expense for this shindig.

As the top floor lit, we gathered our composure and braced ourselves. The doors opened to reveal rolling red carpet that stretched in both directions along the hallway. We stepped forward. Party noises from the right told us which direction to go. We followed the noise to the end of the hall and around a corner. There, we came face to face with two armed guards blocking a suite door. This was our party.

"Good evening, ladies. Are you on the list?" The guard who spoke held a tablet, glancing at it as he awaited our names.

"We were sent by the Dragonfly Agency," I said, all business. Repeating the escort agency name Nova had given me to say, I waited with breath held.

Both men's faces lit up at that. One of them stepped back and shoved the door open. "Welcome to the party. Thank you for joining us tonight."

I was mildly disappointed they didn't card us. We'd come equipped with fake identification. They didn't care what our names were; small talk and introductions weren't what they wanted from escorts.

As we approached the threshold, I noticed the blinking red light strapped to the door frame. That had to be their thermal detection. Seeing it made me swallow hard. I had to put my faith in Nova's locket.

But he'd tricked me once before. Used me as bait. Could I trust him now?

Having no choice but to find out, I followed Dalyn inside, cringing inwardly. The light flashed green as she passed, which apparently was the sign for human. When I followed, the light hesitated, almost giving me a heart attack, er, so to speak. Vampires didn't have heart attacks; we'd already died our human deaths.

When the light blinked green again, I stifled a sigh of relief and sashayed down the short entry hall like I'd never expected otherwise. Grateful, my hand went to the locket around my neck.

We were in.

CHAPTER SIX

T he suite was amazing. Several times the size of my last apartment, I had to pause to take it all in. Warm yellow lit the room, dim enough for a party vibe but bright enough to keep it from feeling like a back-alley dive bar. Four couches were arranged in a square around a coffee table decorated with abstract modern art pieces. An exotic dancer stood in the center, shaking her leather-clad ass. A few people watched, although most of the people on the couches were engaged in conversation. Several real escorts were already keeping the agents busy, doing half the work for us. A pool table with purple felt sat to the left of the sofa set, keeping half a dozen loud men occupied. To the right of the couches, a dining table housed another group playing what appeared to be a drinking game. A staircase next to the table led up to a second floor, where the bedrooms had to be.

"Can you believe this place?" Dalyn breathed in wonder, gawking at the floor to ceiling window. "I've never seen anything like it."

"Well get used to it fast. As far as these guys know, you see ritzy hotels all the time." A quick scan of the place and I didn't see anyone that wasn't human. Not yet anyway. I doubted any of these guys trusted the supes they worked with enough to invite them to such an event.

Finding out just how many of our kind worked for the enemy was a personal interest of mine. I'd never understood why any supernatural would align themselves with an agency intent on the destruction of everyone except baseline humans.

"Right. All the time. Shit, we've been spotted already." Dalyn pasted a brilliant smile on her dark-pink lips. "What's our timeline?"

"An hour tops. Sooner if possible. These guys should be pretty loaded already. Hopefully we find ourselves a talker or two."

I wanted to tell her again to put her safety first if anything happened but didn't get the chance. A middle-aged man with bloodshot eyes and a stumble in his gait approached us with two drinks, shoving one at each of us. Even if I could imbibe, I'd never trust anything one of these dicks handed me.

Both Dalyn and I accepted the drinks with smiles and more sugar than I could muster without wanting to throw up. Actually, vampires didn't vomit either. Not usually. We often wished we could though. Or maybe that was just me.

"Hello, ladies," the drunk Fed hiccupped. "Pleased to make your acquaintance. I'm Jon. Come in and make yourselves comfortable. Preferably right here." Jon slapped both hands on his thighs in invitation.

Yeah, there was that desire to vomit again.

He took turns gaping at each of us, but he seemed to like Dalyn better. Sliding an arm around her shoulders, he led her toward the large picture window, slurring something about showing her the view.

Mouthing, "Do not drink that," as she let him drag her away, I ventured toward the group seated at the couch. One man sat alone, scrolling on his phone. No female companion. Yet. Every woman in the suite was either a stripper or call girl. How had nobody snapped him up yet?

Rounding the couch he sat on from behind, I set my drink on the edge of the coffee table and slid onto the cushion next to him.

He never even gave me a chance to open my mouth. "Gay as hell. Not interested in what you're selling. Just waiting for my Uber to get here." He didn't even glance up as he spoke.

Crap. So that's why he sat alone. I got up to move on.

A man on the adjacent sofa caught hold of my wrist and tugged me down next to him. He had a woman on his other side. "Where are you going?" Whiskey breath puffed into my face, as he leaned in far too close for comfort. "What do you say to a threesome, sexy?"

What I wanted to say included a kick in this guy's crotch. The face of the escort on his other side remained neutral. Unreadable. She'd gotten good at keeping the revulsion off her features. Even her eyes hid it well. She likely had clients that weren't entirely awful, but then there were these guys.

"Whatever you want, handsome." Grinning and bearing it proved harder than I'd thought it would be, and we'd just arrived.

Across the room Dalyn stood near the window, nodding and pretending to sip her drink while the guy who'd greeted us waved an arm at the view of the river below. The balding man next to me tried to tug me closer.

Gaze darting about the room, I sought any opportunity to escape. I couldn't get the right information from just anyone. It had to be the right target.

A tap on my shoulder from behind the couch had me whirling to see who'd snuck up. A good-looking, thirty-something guy with a dazzling smile and a champagne glass in one hand stood there with a brow raised like he'd asked a question.

"You don't mind if I steal you for a while, do you?" he asked, tipping his head toward the handsy Fed next to me. "There's no way in hell this one can handle two women at once. Let's save him the embarrassment, shall we?"

Ignoring the protests of the man beside me, I pushed off the sofa and rounded it to stand face to face with the newcomer. Extending a hand, I purred, "And who might you be?"

He actually had the nerve to leave my hand hanging while he took a drink. When he finally took it, he used it to pull me closer, a move he probably thought was suave but reeked of douchebag.

"I'm Seth, the groom," he said, far too proud of a role he'd already failed at. "Well, I will be next weekend. Gotta sow the last of my wild oats while I can, am I right?"

Everything about this man soured me to him, but I wasn't here to feel sorry for his future wife. "You are definitely right. Yolo, or some shit like that. You can call me Molly."

I had no idea where that name had come from. My acting game was blowing hard. Maybe Tavi's kickass-first-and-beat-answers-out-later approach was better. The subtle approach sucked.

"Can I give you a tour of the place?" Using his glass, he gestured to the second floor. "The view out the window from up there is pretty awesome. Let's get you a drink first." He didn't give me a chance to protest when he fetched a glass stinking of tequila from the bar behind the dining table.

I'd purposely ditched the other drink I'd been given. Dammit. Accepting the glass of noxious fumes, I glanced around, wondering where I could abandon this one.

"Come on." With a hand on my lower back, Seth ushered me along up the winding staircase to the overlooking second floor.

There were three bedroom doors lining a hallway that overlooked the main floor below. Seth guided me over to the glass partition and railing where we could see over. The view of the city was indeed beautiful. The city lights twinkled across the dark expanse of the river.

My gaze fixed on Dalyn and her drunk friend where they still stood chatting near the window. She did a great job of appearing interested, laughing along with him and going so far as to put a hand flirtatiously on his chest. Dalyn was a natural at the sly, seductive spy game. But me? I was growing more impatient and uncomfortable by the minute. Tavi's aggressive approach sounded better every second.

"Gorgeous, isn't it?" Seth gestured to the view, beaming as if he'd created it all by himself.

"It sure is," I agreed, eyeing a nearby plant. "This whole suite is so lavish. You must make a lot of money to be able to throw your party here."

Maybe it was too direct too soon. Cut to the chase didn't work when playing a role. Still, I didn't have hours or days to lure this guy deeper. That kind of espionage wasn't for me. Vampires had no patience for anything but the right moment to make the kill.

"I do all right." Seth's dark eyes roved over me. "You must meet a lot of rich men in your line of work."

Annoyed that he'd sidestepped my remark, I tried another angle. "You have no idea. Some of the richest in the world. Also some of the most dangerous."

"Is that so? Like who?" Eyes narrowed, Seth seemed to be trying to figure me out.

I ran my fingers over my lips in a my-lips-are-sealed motion. "You know I can't share that kind of information. Client confidentiality and all that."

"Of course." Angling closer, Seth slid an arm around my waist. "Do you like dangerous men, Molly?"

The guy fit the bill of tall, dark, and handsome. Too bad for his fiancée, he was a scumbag cheater. I wondered what she thought he really did for a living. Smiling into his stupid face, I resisted every urge to sink fangs into his carotid and leave him to bleed out.

"Dangerous men certainly make life more interesting. They always have some kind of fantastic tale to leave me with. Some of the most fascinating men I've ever met." Not a word of that last bit had been a lie. I did know some amazingly deadly and alluring men. I currently shared a house with many of them.

"So you're that kind of girl." Seth's eyes lit up. Brushing the hair off my shoulder, he dragged his lips over my bare flesh. "You like to hear all about it, do you? I have some stories that would terrify you out of your skin."

With a giggle and an eye roll, I gave him a playful shove, taking care to hide my strength. "Oh please. I've heard everything from alien encounters to drug cartel secrets. I doubt there is anything you can tell me to top that."

As Seth continued to kiss his way to my neck, I swallowed down the ball of revulsion that rose in my throat, almost choking on it. I hoped he gave me something good before he tried slipping a hand in my panties.

"You don't think so?" he murmured against my ear, his breath hot and smelling of hard alcohol. "What if I told you that the monsters of your childhood were real? Vampires who prey on humans, wearing human faces. Not just fiction after all."

Now I laughed, both because he probably expected it and because the man was a damn fool. "Then I'd say you must be on some good shit, and I'd ask where I could score some. If vampires existed, I'm pretty sure we'd know by now."

When I kept glancing down below to keep Dalyn in sight, Seth turned me to face him. Tucking a lock of hair behind my ear, his eyes twinkled like he just couldn't wait to spill more truths that I wouldn't believe.

"They don't want you to know, and neither do we. Me and the guys here, that's what we do. Glorified monster hunters for the government." He mashed his lips against mine before I saw it coming. Cramming his tongue into my mouth, Seth forced a kiss that wasn't sexy in any way.

"So you're like Agent Mulder or something?" I deadpanned, still not taking him seriously. Playing it off like total bullshit was getting me more than if I'd been hanging on his every word.

"I can tell you right now that you're far more likely to run into a vampire or werewolf in this city than an alien. Believe it or not."

Seth drained the last of his drink in one swallow, tipping his head back.

When he wasn't looking, I tipped my glass over the plant pot behind me, lowering the level in my glass. Then I brought it to my lips to leave a smear of lipstick on the edge. Scanning the main level again, I panicked. Dalyn was gone, and so was the man she'd been with.

"So these vampires and werewolves," I said, trying not to seem distracted. "They're just running around the city accosting unsuspecting humans? If that were true, seems we'd notice the dead bodies piling up." My delivery implied that I humored Seth.

Drunk and full of himself, he didn't seem to realize that I was guiding the conversation. Now that I had him talking, I wanted to keep it that way. But if Dalyn didn't reappear soon, I was going to look for her.

"They cover it up. So do we. The general public doesn't need to know this shit. They have enough to worry about on the news each night. If they knew about the things I've seen, there would be mass pandemonium. It's safer for everyone if they don't know." Sliding both hands around my waist, Seth tried to pull me against him.

I resisted. Inside my head I told myself to stay calm. Play along. With a hand on his chest, I held him at arm's length, batting my lashes. "Hold up. Where do these monsters come from? Were they human once? You can't expect me to believe that they all want that life of mayhem."

Seth frowned but appeased me by responding before trying for another grope. "No, I guess they don't all want that. Otherwise they wouldn't be joining our ranks to help wipe out their own kind."

"They do that?" Eyes wide with shock, I took a pretend sip and shook my head in disbelief. "Does it happen a lot?"

His frown deepened. Shit. Was I too obvious? Might be time to excuse myself to the restroom.

"You're just fucking with me, aren't you?" he accused.

I froze.

Then his drunken smile was back in place, and he pawed at me again. "You don't believe a word I'm saying. You're just having a laugh at my expense, aren't you?"

Phew! Relief washed through me. "I might be."

"I think it's time to move this conversation to a bedroom." Grabbing my hand, Seth tugged me along toward the closest door.

"Actually, I need to use the restroom first. I'd like to freshen up a little." And find Dalyn. I was starting to think that the more questions I asked, the more Seth would make me do in order to get my next answer. Perhaps he was onto me, checking to see how far I'd go.

Not knowing how much he suspected, worry was eating at me. If The Circle wanted me to run interference on the street and pull off the occasional hit, sure, that was right up my alley. But this chess game of conversation, of patiently leading him into my trap without revealing myself, it was hell on my nerves.

Not knowing where Dalyn was or if she might be in trouble was worse.

"You can use the ensuite in the room." Not giving me a chance to back out, Seth all but dragged me to the nearest door.

He threw it open and flicked on the light to reveal a basic but nice room, empty aside from a few of his personal items strewn about. Allowing him to close me in there while he tried to get my clothes off was not an option. I excused myself to the attached bathroom.

I locked the door and texted Dalyn. I didn't expect her to answer but had to try anyway. Then I fired off a fast one to Rayne giving him a brief heads up on the situation.

When I emerged Seth held two fresh glasses, offering one to me. "Why don't you slip out of that dress and get comfortable?"

The man wasn't as sly as he thought he was. Because his back was to the mirror over the dresser. In his reflection I could clearly see the sharp wooden stake he'd stuffed into the back of his pants.

My cover had been blown. Or maybe it had never worked in the first place.

Knowing that I was about to make a mistake that might piss off The Circle of the Veil, I tried to talk myself out of it for about three seconds. Ignoring the drinks, I shrugged and said, "Sorry about this Seth. It really wasn't in the plan."

In a swift motion he never saw coming, I grabbed hold of him, hooked an arm around his neck, and squeezed, a choke hold Corr had taught me. Once Seth sagged against me, unconscious, I held tight a few seconds longer before depositing him on the floor. Both drinks spilled in puddles that seeped into the carpet on either side of him.

Working fast, I used his belt to restrain his hands behind him and another from a suitcase in the corner to bind his ankles. After tossing the stake under the bed, I stuffed a ball of socks into his mouth, dragged his limp form into the bathroom, and closed the door.

I slipped out of his room and descended the stairs. Time to find Dalyn and get the hell out of here.

CHAPTER SEVEN

Holding tight to the railing, I used it to keep from rushing to the bottom inhumanly fast. Or any speed other than a casual stroll. I'd rather not run in heels either as they weren't my standard choice of footwear. Since the days when I'd been forced to dress up for the approval and entertainment of my husband and then my vampire sire, I preferred a badass boot with an even heel or a good, supportive running shoe.

Upon reaching the bottom I moved around the perimeter of the room, trying to go unnoticed. Where was my witch?

I could pick out Dalyn's scent in wisps and fragments, mixed in with several other smells. Two dancers outside a closed door muttered in annoyance; that had to be another washroom. It was worth checking out before I tore the rest of the suite apart looking for her.

"Long wait?" I asked the dancers who appeared to be having about as much fun at this thing as I was.

One of them tapped a foot impatiently. "Feels like it's been a while. I think someone's fucking in there. Might be better to just go upstairs."

Gently pushing my way past them, I pressed my ear to the door. Sounds of movement came from inside, muffled by loud music and the murmur of voices. Dalyn was in there with the Fed. I knew it. If anything happened, she could defend herself. Right?

Worry gripped me. Glancing over my shoulder at the dancers who drifted away toward the stairs, I broke the lock with a little telekinetic push. Then without hesitation, I shoved into the bathroom and closed the door behind me before anyone could get a glimpse inside.

And it was a damn good thing I did too.

The mess that greeted me stopped me dead inside the door, my back pressed against it. Automatically, I flipped the lock. Bright crimson painted the white floor tile. The air was thick with blood. Dalyn stood pasted into the corner of the small room, unable to take her eyes off the dead Fed and the gaping hole in his skull.

I reached for the fan switch on the wall next to the light and turned it on, creating more noise. "Are you ok? What the hell happened?"

"He was bragging about his job and what a bigshot agent he is." Dalyn's voice wavered. She inched away from the blood that seeped toward her fancy pink stilettos. "How being hired on for this city is considered a promotion. They're looking for the best of their people. He got touchy feely but he was talking. I thought I could get more out of him, but he got aggressive. Wouldn't take no for an answer. I tried to leave the bathroom, and he grabbed my hair. So I used a spell to throw him off me. But the wasted idiot fell and bashed his skull open on the counter."

Dalyn stared uncertainly at the body. The corner of the counter next to the sink was stained red. Her clasped hands shook. I knew I shouldn't have let her go off with this jackass.

The small confines of the room made the scent of so much blood especially strong despite the running fan. I had to get out of there. Although I'd fed recently, a small room hotboxed with the scent of blood and death had a way of getting under my skin.

A bang on the door behind me made us both jump. "Just a minute," I called. "Someone's sick in here." That seemed to be enough to make the knocking stop. For now. To Dalyn I said in a hushed tone, "We have to get out of this suite."

I pulled my phone from my handbag and texted Rayne to let him know we had a problem on our hands. Since he was our ride out of here, we needed him to be ready whenever we managed to make it back to the street.

"They're going to fucking bust us," Dalyn whisper shouted, tugging nervously at her hair. "How are we going to get out of here without them finding out who we are? There's probably a line up outside the damn door."

"I left a guy tied up in a room upstairs." Reaching for Dalyn, I hooked her elbow and pulled her close, doing my best not to focus on the sound of her rapid heartbeat. "He knew what I was somehow. He was about to pull a stake on me. We have to go now."

Dalyn couldn't tear her wide eyes off the body on the floor. "I can't believe that just happened. I didn't want to hurt anyone."

"Fuck him," I hissed, giving her a gentle shake. "He's the enemy. We save ourselves no matter what. You have to keep it together if we're going to get out of here. Ok?"

With a vigorous nod, Dalyn sucked in a breath and let it out slowly. "Ok, I'm good. What's the plan? Are you good? You look a little… off. Please don't bleed me."

"Don't worry about me. I'm not going to hurt you. The plan is to leave this room and head right for the door. Once we hit the hallway, we take the stairs and meet Rayne where we agreed. Got it?" When she nodded, I added, "Can you do any kind of spell to lock this door? To buy us some time before anyone comes in after we leave."

"I don't know. I can try." She rummaged through her purse, pulling a leaf of some kind out of an inner pocket as well as a small clear crystal.

Setting both items on the floor next to the door, she recited a spell in Latin and snapped her fingers. The leaf caught on fire and quickly went out. Cupping her hands around the smoke, Dalyn used it to draw a wispy symbol over the door, similar to what Nova had done the night I first met him.

"I don't know how long it will hold." She cast one last glance at the dead man on the floor. A shiver shook her. "Let's get out of here."

Easing the door open the tiniest crack, I used my story about someone being sick to chase away the few people waiting. Once it was clear, the two of us slipped out and closed the door behind us. But not before I relocked it from the inside for added measure.

The party had started to thin out as people left for their own suites or grabbed a ride home. Plenty of agents still partied hard though. Enough that nobody noticed our dash for the door.

Or so I thought.

"Stop those two." A shout rang out from the top of the stairs. Seth stood there dazed and angry next to the guy who had found him, pointing at Dalyn and me. "They're supes!"

Without hesitating, I threw the door open, throwing the security guys at the door out of my way with a telekinetic slap. Grabbing Dalyn's hand, I pulled her along behind me, intent on the stairs. Being trapped in an elevator right now wouldn't help us.

Dalyn struggled to keep up as we both ran in ridiculous high heels. Since this wasn't Hollywood, all it did was slow us down. "Get rid of them." I kicked my own shoes off, snatching one up to fling toward the first few men out the door of the suite in pursuit.

Dalyn kicked her shoes off but wouldn't abandon them. Carrying one in each hand, she sprinted barefoot down the hard, concrete stairway. I shoved the heavy door closed behind us and followed Dalyn down the steps.

Being sober with a head start gave us the advantage. Two dozen drunk Feds, all trying to fit down the stairs at once, didn't go as well as they thought it would. One of them shouted to call for backup, and that got me moving faster. Once I sped ahead of Dalyn, I had to slow myself down. I'd never leave her behind.

A shot fired down the stairs ricocheted on its way down. I grabbed Dalyn and pushed her in front of me, blocking her with my body. Another shout followed, one man giving the other shit for firing blindly in a place filled with civilians.

"Keep going," I urged Dalyn, frustrated with how much slower her human body moved.

"I don't know if I can," she panted, stopping to suck in a breath. "How many fucking floors are in this place?"

Above us heavy footsteps still clattered on their way down. Although it sounded like less of them now. Had some gone back to head us off another way? How far could so many wasted Feds get?

"Too many. Keep moving. They're still coming."

Just as we rounded the corner to the next floor down, the door to the hallway burst open and two Feds spilled out. I didn't give them a chance to use the weapons they held. Holding the railing for support, I kicked one of them solid in the chest. He fell backward, tumbling down the stairs to land in a broken heap on the next landing down.

"Go," I shouted at Dalyn, pushing her on ahead. I turned on the other guy, smacking his gun arm down before jerking him close for a killing bite.

I didn't wait to watch him drop. With the taste of his blood in my mouth, I ran down the steps after Dalyn. After making it a few more floors, I grabbed the next hall door we came to and jerked it open.

It was both silent and empty. Pulling Dalyn along as the poor witch struggled to keep up, I pounded the button for the elevator. "We'll take it down a few floors and then get back to the stairway."

Dalyn eyed the numbers counting down overheard. "Please don't make me do anymore stairs, Blaze. Or you'll be carrying me pretty soon."

I used the brief few seconds of safety inside the elevator to check my phone. Nothing back from Rayne. That didn't feel right.

We took the elevator to the third floor for Dalyn's sake. "If you have any spells or anything you can use defensively, have it ready."

She pulled a small black pouch from her purse, gripping it tight. "Got it."

As the elevator slowed, I braced myself. But it opened on an Asian couple waiting for an elevator and nobody else. Together we hurried back to the emergency exit that led to the stairs. Peeking through the small rectangular window, I didn't see anyone.

Ever so gently I eased the door open and listened. The sound of male voices echoed high up. It didn't sound like they were still pursuing us but disappearing into a floor several stories above. They must have found their dead buddies.

When we made it down to the street, we emerged into a parking lot behind the building. No swat team of Feds awaited us. I could have cried with relief. Knowing they were on the way, we didn't have time to hang around.

"Just a little farther," I prodded Dalyn, leading her into the shadows, away from all streetlight. Working the clasp on the locket I wore, I dropped it into my small purse. "Ditch the glamour. They'll be looking for that appearance."

Moving slow allowed us to move in silence, aside from Dalyn's labored breathing as she struggled to catch her breath. Her heartbeat thundered a mile a minute, loud in my head.

Slipping between buildings, cars, and anything else that acted as cover, we made our way down the street toward the agreed upon rendezvous point. Rayne was supposed to be there. Still there was no return message on my phone.

At one point a blacked-out sedan rolled slowly past us as its occupants scrutinized anyone on the street. I'd kept to the shadows, so we were able to watch them from where we stood between two buildings while they searched for us.

Several bars and restaurants lined the busy downtown area. We'd be meeting Rayne in the parking lot of one of the busiest. The dense human presence proved a good way to ensure the Feds couldn't pull any dangerous shenanigans.

When we stood across the busy street from our destination, I said, "On the next break in traffic, run for it. If anyone chases us, we go inside. If not, circle around to the parking lot."

"Got it. I don't think anyone tracked us this far." Hair in disarray and bare feet bleeding, Dalyn held her heels up. She'd stuffed her magic pouch into her cleavage to keep her shoes in hand.

She looked so ridiculous in that moment, I burst into poorly timed laughter. Smacking both hands over my mouth, I muffled the sound until I could compose myself. Nerves could really fuck with a person. "After that van we go. You first. I'll watch your back."

I kept expecting half a dozen government cars to come screeching up on each side of us as we darted across the street. Instead we made it to the other side without issue. Dalyn paused to slip her shoes back on. I didn't miss mine. They'd hurt like hell anyway.

When we rounded the noisy lounge to the lot where Rayne should be, my heart plummeted into my stomach. He wasn't there.

"Fuck," I hissed. Trying a call, it went unanswered.

Knowing that Ghost had gone with him as a second, I called him too. We'd all been given a secure phone to use when running Circle jobs, even those of us who never usually carried one, like the mysterious vampire. He didn't answer either.

"I have no idea where Rayne is." Wary of standing about too long and having the Feds catch up with us, I nudged Dalyn toward a bench near the lounge entry, where people could wait for their cab or ride service. "If they don't show in five minutes, I'll call Smudge and have her send someone else."

With unease hunching her shoulders, Dalyn kept sneaking glances behind and around us. "What if we don't have five minutes?"

CHAPTER EIGHT

RAYNE

Before I left the house to pick up Blaze and Dalyn, Nova pulled me aside. Clapping a hand on my shoulder, he steered me into the front sitting room. Even though he intended to intimidate with his heavy grip, I didn't shrug him off. I wasn't daunted.

"Try to get there and back without any trouble. But if you run into any, I expect you to do whatever it takes to make sure you all make it back here alive." Red eyes glinting with the unspoken promise of violence, Nova's hand tightened on my shoulder. A split second before I knocked it away, he removed it.

"Is that your covert way of telling me to protect Blaze? For one, it goes without saying that I'd take a bullet for her. For two, I sincerely doubt she needs either of us to take care of her."

"You don't have to be an asshole about it," Nova snarled. "I have no doubt that all the time she's been spending in your bed has made you quite loyal to her. I'm counting on that wolf loyalty to ensure you do take that bullet when the time comes."

Yeah, I figured he knew about that. Blaze and I hadn't gone out of our way to hide the time we spent together. Why should we? We were all on borrowed time here. It was a risk we deemed worth taking.

Every night I fell a little harder for her. No point denying it.

"Jealous, Nova? I hear the bitter envy in your voice. But I'm not the incubus she melts into a puddle for with just a glance, so I wouldn't be too quick to think that I have it all. You've got your own thing going with her, and you know it. So back the fuck off." Knowing better than to let the demon lure me into a heated exchange, I turned to leave.

Nova's parting words left me fuming. "If she dies on your watch, you die."

On my way into the garage I slammed a fist through the drywall. Fucking demons and their possessive bullshit. If Blaze knew he'd said that, she'd have been pissed. The woman had existed far longer than I had. I had no doubt she could fuck up anyone who did her wrong. She didn't need me or Nova to protect her.

Nova knew that. His anxiety likely stemmed from his inability to be there himself. Being Circle elite meant that he had duties beyond recruiting and training us rogues. He'd referred to his work at Mayhem House as a punishment, but I'd never asked what he did to get here.

I didn't expect to find Ghost lurking in the dark garage. I tensed when I saw him leaning against the gray BMW.

Without acknowledging my display of temper, he said, "I'm your second tonight. Ready to roll?"

I pulled the keys from a pocket and unlocked the doors with the fob. "Yeah, let's get the hell out of here for a while."

Blaze and Dalyn had arrived at the party twenty minutes ago. It would take me about that long to get over there. My instruction was to wait for them to reach out to me. If I didn't hear from them after an hour, I was to call Blaze. If she didn't answer, we'd be going in. Since it was a bachelor party with drunk federal agents, I didn't expect trouble.

Unless the ladies triggered suspicion.

Ghost sat quietly in the passenger seat. The man didn't say much. But he had a way of moving like a cat through the night, unheard and unseen, that made him a deadly asset to the team. If anyone asked me if I trusted him though, I'd be on the fence. Although he hadn't given me a reason for suspicion, my trust had to be earned.

"Mind if I smoke?" he asked in a raspy voice that sounded like he'd smoked plenty in his time.

"Just open the window." Had to give the guy credit for asking. Most vampires didn't.

We drove through the city toward the downtown core, a relatively uneventful drive spent in comfortable silence. Ghost didn't seem like the small talk type, and that was a nice change for me.

Of course I was curious about the vampire that nobody knew jack about. Not even Blaze who'd had a one-night stand with him. The strength of his power was impressive, and I'd much rather be with Ghost than against him.

Blowing a cloud of smoke out the window, Ghost slid a glance my way, which I felt before he spoke. "Nova's getting pretty hot under the collar over our girl, isn't he?"

His question left me tongue tied and blindsided. Most especially his reference to Blaze as "our" girl. So surprised I had to slam on the brakes to keep from running a red light. "It appears that way. Demons are used to taking what they want. He can't do that with her."

"Fuck no. Not Blaze. He'll learn though. There's no forcing your way in with that one. Too many scars left by those who came before. She's not that person." Taking another drag, Ghost blew smoke rings toward the open window.

His insight into Blaze made me look a little harder at him. As the driver behind us honked their horn, Ghost motioned with his cigarette to the now green light. I hit the gas and sped through the intersection, forcing the BMW quickly up to speed.

"How well do you know her?" I asked, curious because I didn't think she'd told him the things that she'd told me about her sire.

"Not as well as you do," he replied easily, not at all bothered by this conversation. When it came to her, he had the complete opposite reaction from Nova. "But you can learn a lot about a person when you fuck them. Even just once."

Vampires connected with another person's energy on a deeper level than most. I felt it every time I was inside Blaze. She was everywhere, all around me, in my head. They had a way of capturing you fully, completely. They delved deep enough to learn the things that were never spoken aloud.

I nodded, slowing to take a left a block ahead. "Can't argue that."

"Keep signaling left but take a right." Ghost didn't sit up straighter or sound concerned, but he added, "We have a tail."

A glance in the rearview mirror confirmed it. Four cars back a black SUV got into our lane, preparing to turn left. For me to go right, I'd have to cut across the right lane of traffic and hope like hell I didn't cause an accident.

"That didn't take long. They must have cars watching key areas for us." Accelerating toward the left turn instead of slowing, I glanced over my shoulder before jerking the wheel to the right.

The BMW slid across the right lane, cutting off the pickup truck there and just narrowly missing its chrome bumper. Several pedestrians in the crosswalk were forced to jump out of the way. Shit.

From the passenger seat, Ghost chuckled and flicked his cigarette butt out the window. "Nice. They're scrambling now."

I couldn't take my eyes off the road long, but I managed to catch a glimpse of the FPA vehicle as it screeched to a halt and tried to cut across traffic after us. The pedestrian flow slowed them down too.

Speeding toward the next intersection, I checked the time on the dash. I didn't want to be late to grab Blaze and Dalyn. Leaving them without a ride could put them in danger.

"Keep an eye on those assholes." Without signaling I turned at random down a side street, then took another turn down an alley before killing the lights.

"They just drove by the alley entrance." Ghost monitored the activity behind us. "I don't think they saw us. Unless they plan to head you off on the other side."

As soon as he said that headlights beamed bright in our eyes as the SUV rounded the bend ahead, coming right at us. The alley was wide enough for only one vehicle at a time and offered no room to turn around. Slamming the car in reverse, I gunned it backward.

Ghost let out a little whoop of excitement as we shot back onto the street that we'd come from. "Now we're having some fun. Do you want to stop and fight them? Or keep moving? I think we can take them."

We quite possibly could, but I didn't want anything to keep us from getting to Blaze on time. "Let's make that last resort. This thing has more horsepower than what they're driving. I'm sure I can shake them."

I cranked the wheel, put the car in gear, and raced down the street with the black SUV hot on our tail. They did a better job of keeping up than I'd anticipated. I'd been nagging Nova to upgrade our vehicles, and I wouldn't take no for an answer after this.

My own personal ride was one of the fastest machines on the road these days. Maybe it would have to become a bait car instead of a fun luxury ride. The bright color and flashy exterior would easily draw FPA attention and still outrun them.

"Hang a right up ahead. I've got this." Turning in his seat to eye the SUV behind us, Ghost flung a psi ball out the open window.

It hit the front of the SUV, denting in the center of the hood, causing the driver to swerve erratically. Still they stayed on us. Once the first shot had been thrown, they were fast to retaliate.

The passenger stuck a handgun out the window, aiming for our back tires. I swerved to make it tougher, ducking when a bullet nailed the trunk. Adrenaline pumped through me, calling the wolf out. I held tight to the wheel, willing the beast back. "Fuck these assholes."

"Still want to keep moving?" Ghost asked, a sly dip to his gritty tone. "If we stop here we can kick their asses without any witnesses. If you want to keep going, head back downtown. There's too many people this time of night. They won't be able to take any more shots at us."

We wouldn't be able to take any more at them either, but it seemed like the best plan. My phone screen lit up from the bracket on the dash that held it. I thought I saw Blaze's name but had no time to check the message. While I raced through the night, Ghost watched our pursuers, launching whatever attacks he could from the speeding car.

Upon reaching the next intersection, I headed toward downtown's busy main avenue. As we got closer both the vehicular and pedestrian traffic began to thicken. The FPA car lost ground when a truck zigzagged through traffic to cut it off.

The light turned from green to amber, and I made it easily. The Feds didn't have the same luck. The light turned red, and cars in front of them stopped. They were trapped in the pack.

We'd lost that car, but they might have called for another to head us off. We had to get to Dalyn and Blaze before another squad found us.

"That was some seriously sweet driving, brother." Ghost lightly punched my shoulder before pulling out another cigarette. "I'll ride with you anytime."

It took several minutes for my racing heart to slow. A glance at my reflection in the mirror revealed wolf eyes. With the moon growing fuller, the wolf grew more demanding.

"Thanks. Keep watch. They might send another car from a different direction." I flicked on the air conditioner, craving the icy blast on my hot skin. Nothing like a car chase to get the blood pumping, something I hoped Ghost didn't enjoy too much. No doubt he could hear the pounding of my pulse.

A few more blocks without incident and we reached the lounge where Blaze and Dalyn were supposed to meet us. They weren't there. When I checked the messages that had come in from her and saw the missed call, I cursed myself for not connecting my phone to the car's system.

"Do you see them anywhere?" Trying to keep calm while the wolf inside wanted to tear frantically down the street sniffing them out, my gaze darted about.

Ghost sat there unperturbed, scanning the vicinity, puffing smoke like a lazy dragon. After a few moments of consideration, he pointed down the block to a bus shelter. "There."

Waiting impatiently for a row of vehicles to stream past, I pulled back into traffic and blasted toward the enclosure at an alarming rate. People on the sidewalk shouted at me to slow down.

I slammed on the brakes and slid to a stop as Blaze and Dalyn darted toward the car. In a tangle of limbs, they jumped in, simultaneously shouting at me to drive. I didn't need to be told twice.

Although I didn't know exactly how Ghost had so easily felt them out, I was glad he did. The two of them sprawled across the backseat like they'd just run a marathon. Dalyn gasped for breath while Blaze watched out the back window for any sign of pursuit.

"What the hell happened in there?" I asked when I was sure we were in the clear. "You smell like death."

Blaze finally sat back, half relaxed as we made our way back to the house. "Let's just say I think the Feds expected us to send someone. The groom himself lured me to a room to kill me. It's going to be a lot harder to get close to them than Nova thinks."

CHAPTER NINE

Two nights passed without Nova visiting the house. He hadn't come by after our eventful visit to the bachelor party, and try as I might not to overthink it, I couldn't help but worry that he'd run into trouble on his own outing.

Shortly before midnight I went down to the living room where Dalyn and Corr sat on the couch with a mountain of snacks between them, watching their latest Netflix binge show. Since we'd been told via a message sent through Smudge to sit tight at the house and wait on Nova, nobody had left longer than necessary. Food runs and victim visits, that kind of thing. When we did leave it was in pairs at the very least. Assuming the FPA would be looking for the BMW or our SUV, we made a habit of swapping out vehicles as well. Grab one here and ditch it there.

Restless and in need of some action, I ambled over to the easy chair across from the couch, where Corr had left his latest read. Picking up a worn copy of *Interview with the Vampire*, I snickered to myself.

"I've gotta say, I sure am glad that whole coffin bit is bullshit," I muttered beneath my breath.

Corr laughed at my random observation, throwing a piece of popcorn at me that fell short, landing on the carpet a few feet away. "Yeah, I was pretty relieved to find out that silver doesn't do shit to werewolves. Of course nothing was better than learning this thing is controllable. For most of us anyway."

During our time here Corr and I had become friends. Or as close to friends as one could become with a guy that doesn't trust anyone. And who could fault him for that? I couldn't help but wonder what the always-in-control werewolf had done to land himself here if it hadn't involved a reckless snap in judgment. We'd gotten friendly, but we weren't exactly sharing secrets yet.

We talked books, an easy topic for the wolf who didn't speak more than necessary and read constantly. It always got him talking.

And we discussed fight moves, which as a former MMA athlete, Corr knew plenty about. But we had yet to get too personal.

"Don't even get me started." Dalyn paused the TV to fetch a can of pop from the bar near the pool table. "Nothing about my life as a witch comes anywhere close to what books or movies portray. Until now there was a lot less action too."

Rayne sauntered in from the patio, rubbing a towel over his wet hair. Muscles rippled beneath the inked skin of his arms, drawing my eye. It was impossible not to stare. But since the time he'd tossed me in the pool, I tried not to let him catch me.

"Just got a message from Nova," Rayne announced to the room. "He'll be here in ten minutes. We're going out tonight. Something about training. He wants us all ready when he gets here. I'm sending an alert out to the others."

That news had us all moving. After heading back up to my third-floor bedroom, I exchanged satin lounge pants for jeans and pulled my hair into a braid that fell over one shoulder. Since it was a hot summer night, I didn't bother with a jacket or sweater. A spandex tank top and my running shoes kept me comfy but ready for whatever Nova had planned. At least, I hoped so.

By the time I returned to the living room with a yawning Tavi straggling along behind me, Nova already stood among the group. They'd all gathered, standing and sitting while Nova glared from the middle of the room, his arms crossed.

I paused in the doorway, stopped by the sight of him. Black hair loose, spilling past his shoulders, Nova's vicious crimson stare was especially brutal tonight. Although that may have had something to do with the ugly gash beneath one eye and the deep purple bruise that had formed around it.

In my experience demon wounds usually healed immediately. What the fuck had happened to him? There was more though. The black wings usually held so regal and perfectly positioned behind him drooped, like it took more effort than it should to hold them.

"No FPA bullshit tonight. So don't worry about that." Nova's blood red gaze swept over all of us. When our eyes met, I raised a brow. As expected, he didn't acknowledge me. "Tonight you'll be training outside. In teams. To be specific, you'll be hunting one another. Consider this a good time to get really damn good at tracking and evading. I expect that you'll be doing a lot of it in the near future."

Nova split us into teams of two, excluding Ira, the older spell caster who still recovered from a serious leg injury. Corr and I were placed together. We would be hunting Rayne and Dalyn who would be hunting Ghost and Tavi who would be hunting the two of us. So while trying to find our prey, we also had to worry about being someone else's.

"Each team has a different address as your starting point, and you'll be given a general direction to head. That's it. The winning team gets to sit out of the next FPA job." Waving a hand toward the door, Nova dismissed us.

Now that was a prize I could get behind. After the last few outings I could use a break.

"I'll meet you at the front door," I said to Corr, turning to Nova before he could disappear. Not knowing how to start a conversation while my cheeks grew hot, I blurted, "You haven't been around. Is everything ok?"

"Peachy keen, cherry bomb." He chucked me lightly under the chin despite keeping himself just out of reach. "This is nothing. Just leftovers from what happens when one pisses off The Circle's powers that be. I've had worse. Much worse."

That rush of lust I always felt when I looked at Nova now was accompanied by something more. Worry. "What did you do to piss them off?"

The way he held himself made me think he was more injured than he let on. What the hell had they done to him? The FPA might have been the enemy, but The Circle of the Veil were far from the good guys.

"Fucked up a job. Failed to bring them what they wanted. Don't worry, Blaze. I'd never let them do this shit to you." He dragged his thumb across my bottom lip.

I touched the tip of my tongue to it.

Nova pulled away with a curse, taking a step back, like he didn't trust himself alone with me. The soles of my feet burned as I forced myself to stay put when all I wanted was to touch that bruise claiming a large portion of his striking face.

"That's not what I'm worried about," I heard myself say, blabbering from the effect of being around him. "You didn't come around after we hit that bachelor party, and I was afraid—I mean, I was just concerned. I'm glad you're fine." *Smooth move, moron.* I wanted to smack my head against the wall. That feeling grew when Nova chuckled, enjoying my awkwardness.

"I've been better but I've been worse too. Nothing takes the pain away quite like looking at your beautiful face." Something wistful came over Nova's expression as he gazed at me. If he was thinking anything remotely close to what I was thinking, we were just two steps away from trouble.

"I wish there was something I could do to help." I stumbled to get the words out.

"Do you?" Nova challenged, a dark brow raised.

Was this a trick question? Feeling like I'd just walked into a trap, I said, "Of course."

Then he was there, kissing me. Devouring me. Nova's mouth moved on mine, drinking me in. I succumbed to his silent demand, wanting to give him everything. Drowning in the sudden rush of desire, I fell under his thrall.

I didn't stand a chance. Nova wanted to feast on my lust, and that's what he got. With one hand holding the back of my head as he deepened the kiss, the other cupped my ass, pressing me tight to him.

The kiss ended as fast as it had started.

Breaking off, Nova stepped back, releasing me with obvious reluctance. His eyes seemed to glow with a renewed light, like his wickedness level had just been topped up. But most astonishing was how much the bruise marring his face had faded.

Despite the warmth of my cheeks and the wetness gathering between my legs, I felt fine. Better than that. Amazing. Exhilarated and flushed with want.

Enjoying my speechless state of wonder, Nova extended a wing between us, nudging me with the feathery mass. "Now I think the question is, are you ok? Except that I know that you're not, and I know that you won't be until I fuck you in more ways than even the Kama Sutra can dream up. But that won't be happening tonight, and if we're smart, it won't happen ever. You should probably go before I let myself touch you again. If I start, I won't stop until it's over, cherry bomb. Until there's nothing left that I don't know about your body and how to make it mine."

Fumbling to make my tongue work again, I wrinkled my nose. "Is that supposed to make me want to leave? You have seen you, right? Besides, I can't very well go out with drenched panties. You're lucky I just did laundry."

Nova's pained groan was almost my undoing. "You're killing me, woman. Don't tempt me with your wet pussy. I might be strong, but I'm not that fucking strong."

His discomfort was so blatant and palpable that it made my own a little easier to bear. Backing toward the door, I said only, "Yeah, neither am I."

After a quick trip back upstairs to freshen up and splash some cold water on my face, I came back to find Nova on the front porch, barking orders at the others as they left. Gliding up behind him on my way out of the house, I slid a tiny ball of silky fabric from a back pocket and tucked it into his hand as I passed by.

It took him half a second to realize what I'd shoved into his palm. The scrap of royal blue material was a flash of color in his hand as he shoved my underwear into his pocket. Although he maintained an unruffled exterior, his drowning black pupils broadcasted the hunger he possessed for me.

"Watch yourself, Blaze," Nova called after me. "If you want to play that way, expect to lose."

I didn't look back as I crossed the driveway to the silver Mercedes I'd never seen before, where Corr waited in the passenger seat. Taunting an incubus demon with my lust-filled panties was a risky power move if there ever was one. That power could be turned on me in a split second. Still, he hadn't rejected my gift. Nor had he hesitated to feed on my desire once offered. There was only one way this flirtatious dance between us would end. In bed. And the repercussions would follow.

Nova and I both knew that.

CHAPTER TEN

Corr and I drove to an address north of downtown. All we knew was that we were to park the Mercedes in the lot of a twenty-four–hour Tim Horton's and head north from there, toward the large graveyard on this side of the city. Once we were on foot we'd be both the hunters and the hunted. So we could train without issue, the watchdog team scoured the area for FPA activity.

It felt like a fun little exercise. Naturally, I greatly wanted to win. The idea of a night off was encouraging but bragging rights would be nice too.

"Mind if I grab an iced coffee first?" Corr jerked a thumb at the coffee shop.

"Go for it." While he ran inside I tucked the keys under the seat and got out, locking the doors. Smudge would be sending someone to pick it up.

The Mercedes, like many of our rides, had been "borrowed" from the police impound lot. The Circle had a guy there willing to turn a blind eye. We almost always brought them back, which helped ensure the FPA never learned where we got our cars. Changing up the vehicles made it harder for the FPA to track us. We should probably retire the gray BMW; they'd seen it too many times.

When Corr emerged with an iced coffee in one hand and a donut in the other, I snickered. "Nice snack choice. Very hunt appropriate."

We ambled along to the corner and waited for the lights to change so we could cross. Corr chewed a mouthful of donut, casually glancing about, taking stock of our surroundings. "If I've learned anything in the last month, it's that life is too fucking short not to eat the damn donut. And I think I've earned a cheat day."

To emphasize his claim Corr dramatically ran a hand through his short blond hair, using it as an excuse to flex his bicep. The swell of muscle he put on display made me appreciate his choice to wear a t-shirt. I'd seen him work out in the gym enough times to know that the only ink on his upper body was the two black wings outlined in great detail on his back. They were beautiful. Once Corr's shirt came off and he started swinging on that punching bag, I was a smitten kitten. And I wasn't the only one. I'd caught Dalyn ogling the hell out of him.

Since Corr pretty much offered by putting it out there, I helped myself to a feel. Sliding a hand over his bicep, I made an appreciative moan and winked.

"Shut up," he laughed, blushing as he sipped the sweet-smelling iced coffee.

Corr had a laugh that didn't just touch a girl's sweet spot but also her heart. Which made him far more dangerous than one might first assume. It had taken days, several, for him to open up enough to crack more than a grin with the rest of us. He still wasn't much of a talker overall, and aside from Ghost he remained the most mysterious house guest. But he'd started to open up, revealing tiny pieces at a time. Maybe if we both survived long enough, we'd become friends.

"All right, so a werewolf who likes donuts." I paused before stepping off the curb, making sure the traffic properly stopped first. Couldn't trust anyone, especially not some shithead texting and driving through the city at night. "What else do you like?"

We crossed with half a dozen other people, blending in with the small crowd, walking at their pace. "Honestly? My greatest weakness is strawberry Pop-Tarts. Don't ask why. I couldn't tell you."

Having been turned before the snacks were made, I had no opinion either way, but I loved having another nugget of information about the quiet bookworm. Drawing on a dusty old memory, I said, "I used to love these apple tarts my mother made. Funny because I always hated apples. It's probably the one thing I remember most about her. I was pretty young when she died."

Strolling along down the sidewalk, we broke away from the hurrying pack of humans, always rushing to be somewhere. Since we had no idea where the others were, we just kept walking.

"How did she die? If you don't mind my asking." Corr's gentle tone soothed with its friendly warmth.

"She got sick. After a few days she stopped breathing in the middle of the night. It happened fast, so I don't remember much." Not that I wished to remember that time any better than I did. Unfortunately, as I'd gotten older, I'd started to suspect my father had poisoned her.

"I'm sorry. That's rough. I lost my parents in an accident. Both of them. I was fourteen." Corr stared straight ahead as he spoke. As he shared.

When he didn't volunteer more information, I steered the subject in a new direction. "So where do you think the others are? They're going to find us based on the sprinkle trail you're leaving."

A low chuckle rumbled in his chest. He stuffed the rest of the donut in his mouth and pointed at the intersecting streets ahead, a brow raised in question. There were several ways we could go to reach our destination.

"Should we stay out in the open like this?" I asked, doing another scan of the vicinity. "Or try for a little more stealth?"

Sucking back coffee until the straw made that irritating slurp noise, Corr eyed the thinning street traffic. "Let's just keep going a few more blocks, then we'll start to zig zag our path in case anyone is following."

Knowing that Ghost hunted us made me wary, but with Tavi as his partner, we had a chance. He couldn't possibly be as stealthy as usual with her tagging along. As slick as the werewolf could be, she didn't compare to Ghost. He'd disappeared into the night while I was looking right at him.

"Ok, so you like classic books and steamy romance, strawberry Pop-Tarts, and MMA." Tucking a lock of hair behind an ear, I waggled both brows, keeping the conversation light and easy. "What about music? Movies?"

Using the straw to stir the ice in his coffee, Corr considered his answer. "I like a little of everything, but I guess I'm partial to classic rock. Zeppelin and Sabbath type stuff. I actually don't see a lot of movies. Too many based on books that should have been left as books."

Spoken like a die-hard book lover. Having seen Led Zeppelin in concert once, many moons ago, I spent a few blocks telling him about it. When Corr veered left down a side street that led into a residential zone, I followed, trusting his choice.

When I asked him if he liked to write as well as read, he deflected. "Pretty sure it's the vampire who answers questions. I haven't read any books about interviewing a werewolf."

I made sure he saw how hard I rolled my eyes. "How long have you been sitting on that one? Ok, what do you want to know? Ask away."

A pretty bold invitation for sure but I suspected that Corr would never ask a question that he himself wouldn't want to answer. He definitely wasn't going to ask me if I did any writing. Certain now that he did, I was curious what kind of scribblings found their way out of the mysterious werewolf's mind.

Corr ditched the empty cup in a trash bin at the end of a driveway as we passed. "How many years have you been a vampire?"

"Sixty-eight." The number felt strange in my mouth. I tracked that number like the birthday from hell but never said it aloud. Nobody had ever asked. "Twenty-four when I was turned."

"So it was the fifties."

"Early. Elvis hadn't hit it big yet. I still remember when that happened. The human race has been latching onto musicians with frightening fanaticism for as long as I've been around. Only the names have changed." Such a simple question shouldn't have had me focusing so hard on the pop culture of the era, but Elvis Presley's rise to fame made an easier topic than my life at the time.

A prickle along the back of my neck brought me to a halt. Corr paused, raising his nose to sniff the breeze. "Do you feel something?"

I felt the presence of another supernatural. Their energy hummed at a different frequency than a human.

The thing about power was that the more you had, the better you could do such things. Ghost had enough power to easily feel us out. Shit. Was he close? Did he know where we were? Of course, a defensive move would be to shield. I could mentally project a cloak around my energy, to hide it from the vampires, demons, witches, and the like. My shield was only as strong as it's projector though. Without including my wayward blood magic, I doubted I could keep our presence hidden from him.

"I'm not sure. For a moment it felt like we might not be the only ones around. Let's change things up just to be sure." Slipping between two houses, I reached out to Corr. "I can't shield both of us unless we're touching. If that's ok."

Corr's gray-blue eyes fell to my hand, and he hesitated just a split second before engulfing it in his much bigger one. Cold from holding his iced coffee, it warmed quickly as we moved between houses, cut across yards, and darted down back alleys. I did my best to hide us from anyone who might be feeling out the area for supernatural energy.

When we reached a small playground, we paused to take stock of our new surroundings. I felt nothing, but that didn't mean a damn thing. For all we knew the others could be approaching the cemetery from entirely different directions, nowhere near us.

"The cemetery. The real hunt won't be on the streets. Nova expects us to run into the others in the cemetery," I said, certain of it now. "Assuming we don't actually cross paths with anyone until we arrive, how do we want to approach this? Try to get there first? Last?"

Corr gnawed his bottom lip, drawing my gaze to his mouth. Why was I thinking about how his kiss would feel? Damn Nova and the lusty fog he left behind. Yeah, I blamed the incubus.

"Rushing to get there first means racing against Ghost and Tavi if they're thinking that same thing, since Rayne won't be able to move as fast with Dalyn," Corr mused. "But Ghost doesn't seem like the type to rush. What do you think?"

"I think you're right about that." While keeping a tight watch on every side of the tiny playground, I pondered what I knew of Ghost. "Somehow I can't see Ghost showing any of his super stealth secrets to Tavi. If anything, he'll go at her pace, let her set the tone. But I could be totally wrong."

Corr glanced back in the direction we'd come. The coffee shop we'd started at was far behind. "Then we have to take a gamble. I say we get there as fast as we can, but we don't rush in like fools." His hand tightened ever so slightly on mine, bringing my gaze back to him.

Logically I knew there was no double meaning to his words, but they struck me anyway, making me examine him a little harder. "Sounds good. Let's keep going." Moving on kept the moment from turning into something weird.

For me anyway.

I knew Corr was attracted to me. A woman knows such things and a vampire or shifter can smell them. Not to mention the hard-on he'd tried and failed to conceal several times while teaching me defensive groundwork. Still I knew better than to think an attraction was any more than just that.

Attractions were bound to form in situations like ours, forced to live, train, and fight together. Of course I couldn't help but wonder about the strong, quiet werewolf who read all the time and had wings tattooed on his back.

But I already let myself feel for someone in the house. Despite how much I told myself it was just a silly fling, it wasn't. I genuinely cared for Rayne, and the vulnerability of genuine emotion left me wary.

For now, I was happy just to be Corr's friend.

Working as a team, we finally reached the cemetery gates without incident. We needed a better entrance. The cemetery spanned several city blocks, large enough to get lost in the heavy foliage. Driving paths allowed for vehicular traffic, but on foot one could slip through the place unseen. A small forest of trees gave the graveyard a serene vibe, allowing mourners to leave the city behind. We selected a nigh-hidden section of wrought iron fence and climbed over.

Once inside the graveyard we stopped behind a tall headstone to assess the situation. Still holding hands, Corr and I stood face to face, speaking in low tones. Rayne and Dalyn were unlikely to get the drop on us, though one could never be sure with witchy magic. Ghost and Tavi though…

"What now?" I asked, feeling antsy, like I needed to keep on the move.

With a calm smile and a quirk of a brow, Corr said, "We wait."

CHAPTER ELEVEN

CORR

Try as I might to convince myself otherwise, I desperately wanted to know how Blaze smelled. So I might have dipped my head toward hers to get a sniff. Mostly I detected her hair products. I shouldn't be so disappointed. Vampires didn't have their own scent; they created one with whatever aromas they chose.

Maybe humans considered that urge weird. Not a werewolf. Scent was part of imprinting someone on my memory, and such sensory details were vital for survival as a werewolf. We shared a lot of information through scent. With the approaching full moon amping me up, my senses were on overload.

For instance, I could smell Nova on her, his testosterone-heavy musk laden with desire. He wore it like a cologne. Came with the territory I supposed. More often than not lately, Blaze smelled like Rayne. Just one of many reasons why I couldn't let myself continue to feel this attraction to her, though clutching her skin-to-skin only strengthened my desires.

Was I clutching? Fuck me. Easing my grip on her deceptively delicate-looking hand, I forced a tight smile. Why did I suck so hard at just being around people? Around Blaze I felt like I was in the fifth grade again, dorking out over Lizzie Turner, my first crush. She never knew I existed.

Blaze knew. I'd seen her pupils dilate with excitement when we trained in the gym together. She'd made more of an effort to get to know me than anyone else in the house. And I wasn't the easiest guy to get to know.

I'd been a lone wolf long before I'd become one. Once my parents died I retreated into myself and into the fictional worlds that held me captive. The stories helped to push the real world aside for a while. But the more I disappeared into them, the harder it was to come back. I didn't know how to relate to the world around me anymore. Soon it was easier to retreat and avoid.

Then The Circle of the Veil found me. I thought reality sucked before. Well, Mayhem House wasn't all bad. There was Blaze, a rare light in the darkness. All things considered, my fellow housemates weren't entirely awful. Our situation, however, certainly was.

"Ask me another question," I heard myself say. Pressing my back flat against the large headstone we hid behind, I scanned the copse of trees ahead.

"Huh?" Brow furrowed in confusion, Blaze dragged her gaze back to me. We were both on high alert. "Oh, I thought the werewolf didn't answer the questions."

The closest of the cemetery's many streetlights cast its glow on the other side of the headstone, leaving us in shadow. But I didn't need much light to see the way her blue eyes sparkled with mischief.

She nailed me in the ribs with a finger, making me jerk from the sudden tickle. "All right. Keeping it fair, how long have you been a wolf?"

I sincerely doubted she wanted to know that, but Blaze was too nice to pry. Everyone had a story. Some of us, like Blaze, had been happy to share what landed them at Mayhem House.

I wasn't quite so candid. Not because I regretted what I'd done to land myself here alongside the others, but because unlike some of them, I deserved this.

"Six years. Since I was nineteen. I was on the streets then, an easy target." Too easy. I was such an ignorant little dumbass. I still didn't know how I survived my first turn.

After losing my parents, my will to live grew, even if I didn't know how to navigate this world. You learn or you die. That's how it was among those who hunt in the night. Hunting alone for so long had made me numb. Being forced to work with others was changing that, making me feel again. I still hadn't decided if I was cool with the adjustment.

"Ask me something else," I whispered as a lump formed in my throat. Why did I insist on doing this to myself?

At the first sign that I might be feeling anything toward anyone around me, I ran. But I couldn't run now. Not without being hunted and killed by those I served. So I flirted with the idea of getting to know the people forced into this role with me. And the more I thought about getting to know this foxy redhead, the more I was sure it was a mistake.

If Blaze sensed my internal struggle, she didn't show it. She seemed to understand that this was my way of trying to be something I didn't know how to be: friends.

"What did The Circle bring you in for?" came Blaze's throaty whisper, her real question. She watched me in the dark.

I wanted to tell her, or some part of me did. Maybe I would have if the snap of a twig didn't inform us that we weren't alone. Lifting my nose to sniff the slight summer breeze, I searched the night air for information.

Unable to catch the scent of whomever was out there, I started to tug my shirt off. Being able to slink through the headstones on four legs would give me an advantage over two. Reluctantly releasing Blaze's hand, I explained, "Someone's coming. I'm going to shift."

Blaze nodded and politely averted her gaze while I quickly disrobed, leaving my clothes in a pile at the base of the headstone. I dropped to all fours. The shift came over me fast and smooth. Unfortunately, it hurt like hell. At least it took only a few seconds.

Blaze's hand grabbed hold of the tip of my tail as she again blanketed our energy in her protective shield. Our gazes locked, and without the need for words, we agreed. Together we left our shadowed spot behind the headstone and crept toward the sound we'd heard.

As we drew closer I picked up the familiar scent of Dalyn. She and Rayne couldn't be far. The tips of my ears flicked back and forth as I listened for any noise behind us. It would suck ass to get caught off guard now.

We glided between the trees, pausing to search the graveyard ahead before stepping into view of anyone who might be about. No sign of Dalyn. Nose to the ground, I searched for her. Nothing. Nose to the air, the faintest wisp.

Blaze and I exchanged a nod: The coast was clear, so go ahead.

She shrugged. Just as she was about to take a step into the clearing of headstones before us, I caught the hem of her shirt in my teeth and jerked her to a stop.

Seconds later both Dalyn and Rayne came into view. He'd gone wolf as well. They veered toward the small roadway, headed for the shelter of trees on the other side. They were ours and we'd found them.

With no sign of Ghost or Tavi, were we about to win this thing?

Moving in unison, Blaze and I slunk after them. They never saw us coming. We closed the gap with them none the wiser. Until Ghost and Tavi descended upon the four of us like two snakes in the grass, unseen until it was too late.

Coming up on either side, Ghost swooped in on Blaze while Tavi came at me.

Tavi, still in human form, hit me with a body check that was nothing to laugh at. It bowled me over, taking my feet out from beneath me. A surprised snarl erupted from my throat.

Ghost hit Blaze with a telekinetic attack. Nothing heavy, just enough to knock her down. It never should have been a problem. Nothing more than a scraped knee at worst.

Except she fell on the jagged pieces of an old, crumbling headstone.

Blaze's blood on the air was the only warning we got. As she stood up with her cut palm dripping, she shook her head vigorously, eyes wild. The rest of us already scrambled to get out of the line of fire.

A small explosion went off behind me as I dashed through the headstones. Skidding to a stop, I glanced back. Half a dozen headstones had exploded. Chunks of stone lay strewn about. Blaze stood in the center, clenching her bloody hand tight. She appeared unharmed.

Thankfully, so did everyone else. That didn't stop Blaze from lashing out in anger. She directed the next jolt of power at the shrapnel littered about, blowing it into smaller pieces.

"Fuck, fuck, fuck," she shouted, shaking her bleeding hand before wiping it on her pants.

When I was certain the worst was over, I eased up beside her, nuzzling her cut hand with my nose. Blaze's other hand found its way into my fur. Her fingers buried deep in my thick hide, and I leaned into her touch.

Shoulders slumped, she gave a frustrated sigh and motioned to Ghost and Tavi. "Looks like you two win."

CHAPTER TWELVE

A ctually, I'd rather not," I called through the door. "I'm not in the mood."

Leaning against my closed and locked bedroom door would do nothing to keep Nova out, but the idea of holding him at bay made me feel better. After last night's little blunder, I was in a shit state of mind. Since we'd gotten back to the house, I'd been holed up in my room alone.

"You know this door means nothing. Don't you think it might be better if you come out?" The dark lilt to Nova's sensual tone sent a prickle along my spine. "We're going to work on symbol magic tonight whether you like it or not. So we can do this the hard way or the harder way. Your choice."

"Son of a bitch." My head fell back against the door with a thud. "Just give me a minute."

"Starting now."

Nova's sharp insistence had me spinning to flip both middle fingers at the closed door. Knowing that he'd time that minute down to the second, I enjoyed every single one of them as I splashed some water on my face and dragged a brush through my hair. I hadn't needed the minute to get physically ready. Just mentally. But a lifetime of minutes would never be enough.

My confidence had never been so shaken. In the past I'd only had myself to worry about, if and when my blood magic boiled over. Now others stood at my side, people I didn't want to hurt. Too many times I'd come too close. I was a liability and Nova knew it. Why else would he be at my door moments after sunset?

I dragged the door open with a second to spare. Nova stood in the hallway, arms crossed, staring out the open doors of the balcony just off the third floor sitting area, onto the backyard and the pool below. The two smaller balconies that faced the front of the house were in the bedrooms of Ghost and Tavi. Since my room was tucked into the corner facing the backyard, I had no balcony, but I did have a great view, especially when Rayne was in the pool.

"Come on." Nova snapped into motion, ushering me toward the stairs. "You wanted to work on your magic. Well, that's what we're going to do."

"Do we have to?" I muttered, more to myself than to him. When he drew near enough to touch, my feet started moving me quickly down the stairs. It wasn't safe to be that close.

In awkward silence we descended three flights of stairs to the basement. Passing Rayne on the main floor as we turned the corner to the basement, our eyes locked. His concern reminded me why I had to do this. Nova paused to utter an order about keeping everyone out of the witches' library for their own safety.

Not at all reassured by that, I let Nova lead the rest of the way. When the demon closed us in the library, I didn't feel that same sense of panic as last time. No, I felt determined. I cared about my team, and I vowed to do whatever it took to ensure that, of all the dangers they faced every night, I'd be no longer among them.

Nova snapped his fingers, and the fire in the hearth roared to life. "I understand why you're upset about last night, but hiding out licking your wounds won't help you fix the problem. You called me out on my avoidance, but you can't avoid your weaknesses either. If I'm going to help you—really help you—then you have to be willing. And you have to trust me."

"I'm here, Nova. That's as willing as I can get. School me." Throwing both hands wide, I strode over to the fire, close enough to feel its warmth on my face. "I can't make any promises on the trust though."

I glanced over at him in time to see his lips purse and head shake, like he inwardly talked himself out of whatever he wanted to say in return. Instead he held a hand toward the arched doorway that led into the magic circle.

"Shall we?" Without waiting for me, Nova entered the adjoining room.

I watched the flames dance and flicker for a few seconds more before following. Tension gripped me as I stepped into the circle where Nova knelt in the center. Waving a hand over the middle of the pentagram, several items appeared: four iron medallions, like runes with various symbols etched into the metal but nothing that I'd ever seen before; a gold amulet in the shape of a star, a red and orange stone gleaming in the middle; and something that looked like black chalk.

I sank to my knees opposite Nova, listening attentively as he explained each item. Touching the runic stones, he said, "Learn these symbols and they could save you. Draw them anywhere, with anything, then activate them with your blood. They'll channel your blood magic into form. Specific form."

"Sounds too good to be true but go on." I pointed at the black chalk. "Is that what I draw them with?"

"It can be. You can draw them with anything. Your finger in the dirt if necessary. Even your blood itself. But it doesn't hurt to have something on hand." Nova flicked each of the runes across the floor toward me, one at a time, naming them all. "Protection. Grounding. Illusion. Strength. Not that you need more strength. You've already got enough to throw me on my ass." Nova caught my eye and winked.

A wave of lust-driven heat rolled through me. Three feet was not enough distance. If I'd known that one intimate encounter, sans sex even, would cause such longing, would I have still done it?

"And the amulet?" I prodded, noticing that he hadn't addressed it.

He touched a fingertip to the top point of the star, catching it by the strip of leather it hung from and lifting it up. Less than two inches across, the star's stone seemed to gleam with an inner light. From deep red layers to brilliant orange, the gem embodied fire.

"It's my talisman," Nova finally said, short and clipped. "Wear it. Carry it in a pocket. Hell, throw it away if you prefer. But if you ever need someone to have your back, you can use it to summon me." Swinging the pretty star toward me, Nova's face was void of all expression in expectation of rejection.

I took it, letting the star lay in my palm. Unable to resist the call of its beauty, I ran my thumb over the stone.

"It's a fire agate," Nova said softly, watching me marvel at the talisman. "Rub the stone and I'll come."

"It's beautiful, Nova. Thank you." Knowing that he'd never have given something so personal and powerful away to just anyone, I tucked the talisman into my bra, enjoying the way his gaze followed. "So what now?"

I had to ask the question a second time before Nova tore his eyes away from my cleavage. "Now we really get started. Once you get to know the symbols, you'll be able to draw them in a heartbeat. I recommend using your palm."

Using the chalk, Nova scrawled one of the symbols on his palm: illusion. Since they were all relatively simple, it took no time at all. The atmosphere grew heavy when he pushed forth a bit of his magic. A small white rabbit hopped through the circle and disappeared into the wall.

"The symbol helps focus the magic into a specific outcome, so it can't run wild. Now you try." Nova held out the palm he'd just marked, and a small dagger appeared in his hand. He offered it to me, handle first. "Just a shallow cut. Start small."

I faltered, unable to take the dagger. "How am I supposed to have even a few seconds to draw a symbol when sometimes the effect is immediate, the second my blood spills?"

Nova's crimson gaze narrowed. "Sometimes? So it's not always immediate?"

"No, I guess not." Upon thinking back, I slowly shook my head. "There's been several times when I managed to hold it off. But it's like trying to hold back a fire raging out of control. I can't hold it long."

"But you can hold it?" Nova pressed, leaning closer. "How do the circumstances differ at those times?"

"I don't know." My mind went back to the night our team had intercepted an FPA prisoner transfer.

Rayne's claw had cut a gash in my arm, and I'd ran for the road, trying to get closer to the Feds before my magic went off like a bomb. And I'd done it. Just barely. Yet other times, the moment my blood surfaced, the magic exploded.

"The night of the transfer, I was afraid of hurting my own people, so I ran toward the Feds." Memories continued to turn, bringing forth the night I'd killed Remington. The magic had burst out, driven by panic and desperation. No control. "But when I'm backed into a corner, it just happens, and I can't control it."

Tilting his head to one side, Nova studied me while tapping a finger against the illusion rune. "Now we're getting somewhere. Try a small cut, here in a controlled setting. Keep calm while you draw the rune in your palm. See what happens."

"And if the magic goes wild?" I asked, nervous as I took the dagger.

"It's contained inside the circle. Don't worry about me. I can take it."

Despite Nova's assurance, I couldn't resist taking a jab at him. "But can your ego?"

The glare he shot me was downright smoldering. If he'd been going for sinister, it was a massive fail. "Watch it, cherry bomb," he snarled, flashing beastly fangs. "There are no witnesses this time."

A shock of desire spread out from my core. Anyone in their right mind would find Nova terrifying. He was a strong demon warrior with power that made me weak in ways I hadn't known possible. My yearning for him had made its way into my dreams as well as my waking moments. I just wanted to touch him and make this longing go away.

Instead, I used the small blade to poke a tiny hole in the tip of a finger. Just enough to bring one drop to the surface. Anything to break through the lust fog in my brain.

The tiny sting wasn't nearly painful enough to dull the sparks between my legs, but it did get my adrenaline flowing. Fear crept in to steal over me. Could I do this? Before I could hesitate, Nova shoved the chalk into my other hand, holding it tight, guiding it quickly through the three slashing lines and the circle surrounding them.

"Make a rabbit," he instructed. "Just like mine. See it in your mind."

The rush of blood magic that bubbled up was small but strong. Having no choice but to obey, I frantically pictured a white rabbit just like the one Nova had conjured. As he'd said, the magic followed the path laid out by the symbol's projection.

My rabbit burst into being. There was no other way to describe how it arrived, like it had been forcefully yanked into our dimension from another. It tumbled and rolled before hopping up and coming straight at me. Red eyes glowed from within black fur, as a mouthful of vicious little teeth latched onto my ankle.

"Ouch, motherfucker." I shook the rabbit off, violently flinging it out of the circle. It promptly disappeared. When I found Nova laughing, my temper flared and I jumped to my feet. "Good thing you didn't tell me to imagine a fucking rottweiler. What the hell was that, Nova?"

He rose as well, keeping his distance. Wings tucked in tight against his back, his laughter faded. "That was you panicking. I'm not going to pretend to understand your fear, but if you'll let me, I might be able to help you overcome it."

Arms crossed tight as if it would protect me from him, I scoffed. "Doubtful. Unless you can remove the panic trigger from my head."

"Remove it, no. But I can steer you through. Keep you calm." Nova spoke as if he wasn't proposing a move that would take the sensual craving from uncomfortable to irresistible.

Not ready to allow him that close, I countered with a question I'd been sitting on since he'd first mentioned using symbols with my magic. "Is this really necessary? How is learning demon magic supposed to help a vampire?"

Nova's gaze dropped to the pile of trinkets on the floor. Did he just avoid eye contact? He damn well did.

Just when I was about to demand to know what he was hiding, he said, "Only demons have red auras."

All sound drained from the room, leaving me with a ringing in my ears. Nova's words echoed inside that ringing, drilling deeper with each repetition.

Vampires were descended from demons, as the old stories went. There was more than one origin story, the most common being that vampires were created from the darkness by demonkind, as an affront to God, turning people into monsters who preyed on his precious humans. Other tales were more fantastical, more like fairytales. In one a king struck a deal with evil itself to preserve his daughters forever, the first vampires.

It didn't matter which story was true; either way, I was no demon.

"What does that mean?" My tongue felt heavy as I tried to speak around the lump in my throat.

Hearing the crack in my voice, Nova jerked his head up. "I'm not sure yet. If you want me to help you find out, I will. But I'm going to go out on a limb and say there's more to you than you think, Blaze."

He huffed in soft irritation. "Don't look so scared. It doesn't have to be a bad thing."

"It doesn't sound like a good thing. And I'm not scared. I'm… frustrated." It didn't sound convincing, but I wasn't going to admit fear to a demon. When several long moments passed and he hadn't said anything, I raised a brow. "What?"

"Nothing." He shook off whatever had held him in its grip and took a careful step closer. "Let me help."

I didn't want Nova's help, but I needed it. Knowing that I might regret it, I relented. "All right."

He motioned for me to come back and sit down in the middle of the circle. I did so, with great reluctance, sitting cross-legged across from him. Coming back into his field of energy felt like walking out of a snowy night into a warm house: welcoming, inviting. Like I could just fall right in.

So I did. Only as I allowed the soothing sensation of calm to come over me, I realized it was all Nova. Even though he'd slipped me some of this calming effect before, it was impossible to detect until I'd already succumbed.

"This feels like cheating," I muttered.

Nova reached over to take one of my hands, and I stared in detached wonder. Turning my hand over, he redrew the smudged illusion symbol in my palm. When he picked up the knife, I didn't twitch or flinch. I felt no fear. Just calm. Like I didn't have a damn care in the world.

"You can draw the symbols beforehand in something more permanent if you wish," he spoke in low tones that had me analyzing every note and lilt of his voice. "You'll figure out what works best for you. Now picture another rabbit. Sweet this time. White and cute as fuck."

Pressing the tip of the blade to my finger, Nova didn't pause or hesitate. He jabbed my finger, so the blood welled up thick and fast.

I gasped but did as instructed.

The rabbit that hopped through the circle this time was white and fuzzy, harmless. No fangs or murderous temperament. It hopped over to sniff my foot before disappearing without incident.

Nova didn't let go of my hand, and I couldn't bring myself to pull away. Not when all I could think about was climbing onto his lap and riding him until sunrise.

In a last-ditch attempt to distract myself, I asked, "What am I going to do with a bunch of fake rabbits, Nova? I doubt the FPA will run screaming from ankle-biter bunnies? Show me something I can really use."

His sexy chuckle seemed to be everywhere, all around me. That damn incubus vibe. It was like taking a hit of illicit narcotics. My entire body broke out in goosebumps despite how incredibly warm the room felt.

"Hey, I chose rabbits to start you small. Once you can control it, it can be anything you want: a pack of wild dogs, a fire-breathing dragon, a mirage in the desert. The choice is yours." Nova's smile faded, and something almost sinister crept into his expression. "But if you want bigger, we'll go bigger."

A flutter in my chest threatened to steal my breath. "I want control of my magic. This madness has gone on too long."

Every passing second the room swelled with the rising tension between us. When Nova stroked a thumb over the back of my hand, I expected the entire library to combust under the pressure. How did he manage to make such a small touch feel so deep and intimate?

"Try this one." He picked up the grounding rune, turning it so I could see the symbol clearly. "If you master this one, it will at least keep you from losing control at the wrong place and time."

"Shit, ow." I jerked when he cut me, spilling enough blood this time to cause a rivulet to drip down my finger and splash a drop onto the floor.

The blood magic welled up along with it, but with Nova's calming influence, I felt no panic, only a strange expectation of my magic's arrival. My entire body buzzed with the power that filled me. When it didn't immediately run amok, I rushed to scribble the symbol on the back of my hand.

Once I slashed the last line through the triangle, the magic obeyed the symbol's unspoken command. A spiral of red energy shot toward the center of the circle to be consumed by whatever magic kept all spells' effects from leaving this chamber. The grounding freed me of the load called forth by my shed blood.

"Outside this room, the magic will ground out into the earth. Best place to shoot a load this side of the veil, so to speak." Nova snickered at his own crude choice of words.

"That's all well and good, but there won't be time to mark myself or anything else with demonic symbols," I insisted, shaking my head at the chalk I held. "Not if the FPA are pointing guns in my face."

The weight of Nova's watchful gaze had me glancing up to find him staring at my hands, at the blood that had dripped down one finger. "Blood magic using symbols isn't ideal for every situation, you're right. It's for activating the spell within the rune at your leisure. However, you'd be wise to learn how to use it. I can promise the day will come when you're glad you did. Still nothing will help you gain ground with your magic as much as mastering your panic response. You know that's the real issue here."

I wiped my bloody fingers on my pants, hating the way the truth sounded on his lips. "I don't need you to tell me that. But I appreciate what you're trying to do here."

I truly did. In a situation like what Dalyn and I had been in, being able to use symbols to guide my blood magic in a specific direction might have been helpful. But nothing would help if I didn't deal with my past. Nova couldn't help me with that.

Waving a hand at the runes on the floor, I started to get up again.

"Don't go." He rose with me. "I can help, but you have to let me in."

If I hadn't had his soothing vibes lulling me, I'd have been angry. Just hearing him say that made me want to let down my walls and expose all my inner self to Nova. Now that was the real illusion here, savage bunnies be damned.

"I can't do that." Closing my eyes, I tried to shut down the nagging need for his incubus touch. The longer we were together, the stronger it grew. "You forced me to be here. You used me as bait on one of my first nights. You're a demon who works for The Circle of the Veil. For that matter you're asking me to give you something that I haven't given to anyone for a very long time."

"What about Rayne?" The question seemed especially loud in the quiet room. When my eyes snapped open, Nova was regarding me not with accusation but curiosity. "Looks like you've let him in."

I didn't detect any jealousy, not that there should be any. Nova and I had no connection other than lust. That simply wasn't enough to build on.

"I have, somewhat," I admitted, feeling like the few feet separating us had grown suffocatingly close despite neither of us having budged. "He's been a good friend, helped me settle in. Do you have any idea what it's like for us here? All we have is each other, and we could lose that at any time."

Nova raised both hands in surrender and took one step forward. The heat level in the room rose several degrees. "Simmer down, firecracker. No judgment. I know how precious time is to you all right now. That's why I'm trying to help you before it's too late. I just wish you could trust me too. Honestly, if I were in your shoes, I'd tell me to go fuck myself. But I understand the trials of being under The Circle's thumb more than you know."

The call to touch him, to feel him, surged. Since the second we'd walked into the library I'd been fighting it. I couldn't fight anymore.

"Then tell me," I said, breathy and weak, trying and failing to keep from throwing myself into Nova's arms.

He saw it all over my face. Muscles in his jaw worked in frustration. "Don't look at me like that; I can't keep resisting you. If you think The Circle is a threat now, you don't want to find out what will happen if they learn I've crossed any line with you. I'm here as a punishment, just like the rest of you. Even the elite have rules to follow."

Was this crazy demon just fucking with me now? The ridiculousness of this entire scenario had my temper sparking. "Are you kidding me?" We were so close I shouted in his face. Still I held myself back. I refused to be the first to break. "One minute you want me to let you in, and the next you're pushing me away. What the hell do you want from me, Nova?"

Nova's piercing gaze darted about my face. Forehead furrowed in frustration, he surprised me by whispering, "I wish I knew."

His lips were on mine before I could be sure which one of us had leaned into it first. Not that it mattered. The rush of touching him made it impossible to think of anything else. I threw my arms around Nova's neck and jumped up to wrap my legs around his waist. His hands on my ass supported me as I swirled my tongue alongside his, happily burning in the incubus fire.

The desire for him roared into a blazing inferno from a spark that had ignited weeks ago, fueled by lust. I didn't trust Nova—I wasn't even sure I liked him—but I desperately wanted him.

He backed me up against the wall, pressing me to it as he hungrily kissed me. The threat of The Circle's wrath didn't scare me. Not with Nova's mouth on my neck, his vicious fangs scratching my skin. Nothing mattered but finally having him inside me.

When he pulled back to peer into my eyes, I saw his resolve falter. Nova wanted it as bad as I did, maybe even more. He also had more strength to resist the temptation.

"You have no idea how bad I want this, but if there will ever be a right time, this isn't it." He kissed me again, small and chaste this time, before lowering me back to the floor and disentangling himself from me.

I gaped at him, bewildered. Was this damn demon trying to drive me mad? "Nova," I began, stopping when he raised a hand to cut me off.

"Don't ask me to stay," he pleaded, backing away like I was the one to be feared. "Or I won't be able to stop myself from taking you right here and now. You'll hate me later if I do. I'm sorry, cherry bomb." The sound of rustling feathers accompanied his departure.

Nova left me standing there in the ritual room, lips parted and thighs quivering. Who even does that? An evil incubus demon, that's who.

Slowly I sank to the floor, sucking in deep breaths in a faltering effort to clear my head.

But try as I might, there was no stifling the fire Nova's incubus touch had ignited.

CHAPTER THIRTEEN

The craving Nova had left me with refused to fade. It drove me from the library in search of a willing partner to help ease the pain. Because that's what it became, a painful need so demanding and so starved that it would not be silenced. Not anymore.

I flung open the library door to find the hallway dark and quiet other than the gym lights at the opposite end. The squeak of shoes on the polished floor drew me in that direction. Hoping to find Rayne beating on the punching bag or lifting weights, I instead found Ghost.

No doubt he could do a lot of damage in a physical fight. Like a foreboding vampire god, he stood shirtless in sweatpants and runners, golden brown skin taut over the hard abs that drew my eye. Holy damn, Ghost was gorgeous. I just wanted to lick him.

Leaning in the doorway to the gym, I watched him pound the crap out of the punching bag. He knew I was there. Not for a second did I think it would be that easy to sneak up on Ghost.

He turned to nail me with a dark stare that smoldered with intrigue. He would've sensed my overexcited energy coming his way. "What's up, doll? Come to work out some tension?"

"You could say that." Pushing away from the threshold, I moved toward him, a prowl in my step. "I can't take this fucking place anymore, Ghost. It's making me crazy."

"Is it the place though? Or is it Nova? You let him get too close." His tone held no judgment, no emotion regarding Nova at all. He watched me come closer, his dark gaze drifting over me.

"I know." The throb between my legs demanded to be satisfied, and I knew Ghost was more than capable.

"And you want me to scratch the itch he left behind, do you, baby girl? With a vicious grin slipping over his handsome features, Ghost's smoky voice encouraged my need for release.

Though I slipped him a coy smile, I felt like a seductive temptress. "Yes, please."

It wasn't like I hadn't sought out lovers over the years. Of course I had. But my desire had never been so desperate. Dark need, created by an incubus demon who would only make my life hell if I let him get any closer, wracked my body.

Ghost's eyes narrowed, and he came to meet me in the middle of the gym. Every move he made screamed with predatory intentions. "I'd love to. Want the wolf to join us?"

I stared at him stupidly while my brain replayed his question a few times. Did I hear what I thought I heard. "Rayne?"

Enjoying my sudden awkwardness, Ghost chuckled. "Why not? Seems only fitting."

Hell yeah it did. While taking Rayne's blood after my magic had drained me, the three of us had been on the brink of an encounter when Nova burst in, destroying a fantasy I hadn't known I'd had until then. I decided it was only fitting to have both Rayne and Ghost satisfy this unyielding want Nova left gnawing at me.

"I'd love for him to join us, if he's up for it."

"He was ready and willing last time." Ghost wrapped a strong arm around my waist and dragged me close, squeezing a little squeal from me. He didn't kiss me though. Taking my hand with the cut fingertips, he sucked one into his mouth, tasting me.

Getting Rayne on board took little more than me poking my head into the kitchen where he stood drinking and chatting with Dalyn and Retta. Once I caught his eye, I hooked a finger in invitation, and he followed me upstairs.

"Did Nova leave?" he asked as we reached the second floor. "Did everything go ok?"

"Yes and not really." I took Rayne's hand, sliding my fingers between his. "He left me a little… uncomfortable, for lack of a better word."

"Pretty sure there are several better words," Rayne teased, amber eyes going solid wolf. "Frisky. Turned on. Horny."

"What about randy? That's kind of a weird one." I smacked his stomach, laughing despite the way I eyed him with unashamed want. "Speaking of weird, this might be but there's no harm in asking, right?"

We reached the third floor and my closed bedroom door. Shoving it open, I stepped inside. Ghost sat on the couch by the fireplace with an unlit cigarette tucked between his lips. Once Rayne saw the vampire, relaxed and waiting, he nodded in understanding.

Rayne closed the door and flipped the lock. "You never have to ask. The answer is always yes."

That made me whimper in need. The twinge in my stomach and the dampness in my underwear demanded attention from the men. Feeling like a cat in heat, I had half a mind to get on all fours and see who got behind me first.

My cheeks grew hot at the thought. Nova's power was dangerous no doubt. If it already had this effect on me, how much worse would it be if he'd stayed? I shouldn't have wanted to find out, but some twisted, dark, depraved part of me fantasized about being taken by him.

"Rules?" Ghost's libido-stroking rasp drew both our gazes to him. Twirling the cigarette between his fingers, he eyed us each in turn.

Rayne peeled his shirt off and tossed it onto the dresser. "I'm all about the ladies, so it's all about her for me sexually. As for bloodletting, I'm cool with either of you taking a nip but only a nip. Don't get carried away. Blaze?"

I tried to remember if I had any boundaries. Nova's influence made it feel like boundaries were for cowards, and I wanted it all. But that wasn't really me. Was it?

I knew I was staring at Rayne's tattooed physique, but I couldn't stop myself. "Um, I don't know. It's hard to think clearly at the moment. I can take some pain with my pleasure. No backdoor entry. Otherwise, I'm here for the taking."

Where did that come from? Not at all shy about my sexual desires, I wasn't quite such a wanton sex goddess about it either. *Damn you, Nova.*

When it was Ghost's turn, he tossed the unlit smoke onto the coffee table and dimmed the tall lamp next to the couch, so it bathed the room in soft light. "I'm here for you, baby girl. Whatever you want."

Such an easy-going response from Ghost didn't surprise me. Yet I didn't expect him to grab me by the waist and push me toward Rayne while pressing against me from behind. My hands splayed on Rayne's bare chest, and I peered up at him in excited wonder.

Ghost gathered my hair in a hand and twisted it around a fist, tugging it aside. A prickle of anticipation caused me to suck in a breath when he kissed the back of my neck. My eyes widened, and Rayne laughed softly before claiming my lips with his.

The sensation of being trapped between the two of them had my arousal running on overdrive. I'd tear a strip out of anyone who dared to interrupt now. I kissed Rayne with unspoken demand, needing to appease the ache between my legs. Ghost pressed his erection against my ass, and I wriggled against him.

Rayne paused from plundering my mouth to tug my shirt off over my head. That's when I remembered the talisman Nova had given me. I slipped it from my bra and set it on the dresser. Neither of them commented on the item.

While Rayne released the clasps of my bra, Ghost slid my pants and underwear down my legs. They had me naked in no time. Ghost turned me to face him, a hand curving around the back of my neck as he jerked me close, crushing his mouth to mine. From behind Rayne's hands grasped my hips.

The men steered me over to the bed and laid me in the center of the large mattress. The scent of fresh laundry puffed up around me.

"One more rule," I said, watching them finish stripping down next to the bed. "No stopping due to interruptions of any kind. Unless the house is on fire. And even then I might not make an exception."

Ghost grabbed my foot, raising it up so he could lean in and kiss the inside of my ankle. That subtle sensation managed to be insanely erotic. "Don't worry, doll. We'll take good care of you."

He slowly kissed his way up the inside of my leg, stealing my voice when I felt the tip of his tongue glide over the curve of my knee. The mattress dipped as Rayne got onto the bed beside me. Already rock hard, he cupped one of my breasts before sucking my nipple into his mouth.

As the heat of Ghost's mouth reached my inner thigh, a small gasp escaped me. When he nudged my legs apart to expose my needy pussy, I trembled in impatient anticipation. Knowing how bad I wanted it, Ghost took his time kissing his way up each thigh. Only when I was ready to burst out of my skin from the exquisite anguish did he stop with the tease.

He dragged his tongue along my wet slit, and I almost hit the roof. The sensations were stronger and more intense than usual.

Ghost's tongue flicked over my clit, and I almost came instantaneously. What the flying crap had Nova done to me?

Rayne's mouth was on mine. Gently kneading my breasts and pinching my nipples into taut points, he kissed me with a demanding fervor. I could feel the wolf within him lurking so very close beneath his skin. It shone in his eyes when he pulled back to gaze down at me. Those gleaming gold wolf eyes raged with desire. And something more. Emotion. Affection.

Afraid to see anything deeper, I touched his cheek, drawing his mouth back to mine. Nova had already asked something of me that I couldn't give. I didn't want that to happen with Rayne too. So I buried myself in the sensations of him, his scent of man and wolf, the possessive way he kissed me, and shoved all higher thought aside.

Ghost's oral attention grew in intensity. From gentle and delicate to demanding and carnal, he licked me with an aggression I could feel in my bones. When he slid two fingers into me, I couldn't have held back if I wanted to. I came with a loud moan that Rayne muffled with another kiss.

But Ghost wasn't content to stop there. Hands on my hips, he got me up onto all fours. Kneeling behind me on the bed, he held my ass with one hand while licking me again. His tongue flicked my now too sensitive clit, and I jerked away, flushing with heat when he chuckled wickedly.

Facing Rayne, I wrapped my hand around his hard shaft, stroking it with familiarity. I knew how he liked to be touched. And I knew how much he loved watching me suck the entire length of his cock into my mouth. Holding his gaze, I ran my tongue around the head teasingly before devouring all of it. Rayne's groan of pleasure trailed into a growl that made me eager for more.

Behind me Ghost adjusted his position. The velvet soft head of his cock rubbed against me, and a trill of excited adrenaline hit my veins. Both hands holding tight to my ass, he slid inside me.

I was pretty sure nothing I'd ever experienced in my life so far had felt this fucking amazing. With Ghost fucking me from behind and Rayne gently thrusting into my mouth, I was overwhelmed with the way my senses fired, overloaded by the two of them.

Rayne slid a hand into my tresses, holding my hair aside so it wouldn't obstruct his view. He stroked a finger down the side of my face in a gentle caress, and I leaned into the familiar comfort of his touch.

Every thrust that buried Ghost to his balls had me moaning around Rayne's swollen cock. Though my connection to the two of them right then was physical, I felt it deeper than that. These two men had come through for me in my time at Mayhem House. They'd proven themselves to be worthy of the one thing Nova asked for, the one thing he had not yet earned: trust.

I trusted the two of them to have me between them, at their mercy, taking what they gave me. That alone was a revelation. In an eye-opening moment I saw clearly how truly free I was, even within the walls of The Circle's prison.

Not only did I trust the two men staking claim to my body, I'd started to fall for Rayne. Feelings had bloomed despite my best efforts to starve the seeds and crush the leaves that sprouted. Did he know that I felt something I didn't know how to feel?

Ghost withdrew, allowing Rayne to change up our position. The werewolf chose to turn me, rolling me onto my back so my head was now by Ghost. Shoving my legs apart, Rayne knelt between them and thrust inside me, his thumb rubbing lazy circles on my clit.

Sitting above me, Ghost propped my head on his lap before running his hands through my hair and down over my breasts. My back arched up into his sensual massaging touch. I reached above my head to grasp his straining hard on, pumping it with a hand.

The sound of Rayne's steady heartbeat reverberated in my ears, louder as his pace quickened. Through his myriad aromas of male pheromones, sex, and sweat, I could still pick out the powerful tease of werewolf blood.

I wanted to taste him while he was inside me. With one hand above me I stroked Ghost closer to orgasm. The other I used to grab hold of Rayne's wrist, pulling him closer so I could run my tongue over the throbbing pulse there. His pace momentarily faltered.

The press of my fangs against his skin brought the beast out. Not only were Rayne's eyes wolf, he boasted fangs bigger and scarier than mine. Claws tipped the fingers of his hands. Although he was careful, a slight sting between my legs only enhanced my pleasure. Ghost's dark, watchful stare rested heavily upon us both.

My fangs pierced the werewolf's vein, and a spurt of blood rushed to fill my mouth. Rayne's thrusts grew harder and faster as I sucked at the bite. Holding his primal gaze, I pulled back and offered his bleeding wrist to Ghost.

The two of them shared a look as Ghost silently asked permission despite having already received it. When Rayne made no move to stop him, the vampire swirled his tongue over the punctures.

With a wolfish groan, Rayne came almost immediately. His frenzied thrusts pushed me over the edge, and I found myself twitching around his cock, a cry on my lips. Ensuring Ghost wasn't left out, I pumped him faster, bringing him along with us. He angled himself to come on my chest, avoiding my face and spattering my breasts instead, a move I appreciated.

After sauntering back from the bathroom with a damp washcloth, Ghost gently cleaned me up before grabbing his pants from the floor. Leaning down to kiss me where I still lay sprawled on the bed beside Rayne, he asked in his low smoky tone, "Feel any better?"

I considered the question. The ramped up supercharged sex drive Nova had left me with had been satiated for the most part. But this little craving niggled below the surface, although I suspected only Nova himself would satisfy that.

"You have no idea." A relaxed smile stole across my face. I didn't think I'd ever felt so perfectly content.

"Good. Always here for you, doll." Slipping his pants back on, Ghost retrieved his cigarette from the coffee table and tucked it behind an ear. He returned to me, leaning down to press a kiss to my lips that tasted of Rayne's blood. "You two look like you want to get into cuddle mode, so I'll leave you to it. Until next time." Ghost winked and ambled toward the door.

So he wasn't a cuddler. Interesting. Or maybe he was under the right circumstances? The mysterious vampire left me more curious about him every time we interacted.

"Want to hit the shower or stay here a while?" Rayne asked when I snuggled in against him.

With my head on his chest, I listened to the thundering beat of his heart, letting it lull me into a pleasant state of calm. Knowing such moments were short lived, I said, "Let's just stay here."

CHAPTER FOURTEEN

NOVA

Hands clenching the railing, I stood on the balcony of my other side penthouse apartment, staring at the deep purple sky. Far in the distance a winged creature flew toward one of the two moons, a dragon most likely, though it was too far away to make out.

Since leaving Blaze in a puddle of desire back in the library of Mayhem House, I'd been trying to talk myself out of wanting her. I'd come straight home for a cold shower that had done nothing to quench the burning need I had for that woman. Why couldn't I get her out of my head?

It had been an incredibly long time since I'd felt anything for anyone. Emotions had no place in an incubus's life. Too complicated and messy, turning what should be nothing more than a quickie orgasm in the garage into a moment I couldn't stop replaying in my mind.

Blaze's sexy fucking moans rang in my ears. I could still feel the way her pussy clenched around my fingers. Fuck me, why should she be any different than anyone else? I didn't do feelings, and I sure as fuck didn't do love. What I felt for Blaze wasn't love, but it was a shit ton more than I was used to.

I hated every fucking second of this.

"Get off the railing, Nika," I snapped at the black furry, winged creature walking the thin rail without care. "Your pitiful wings would barely slow your descent if you took a fall. I'd rather not have to scrape your carcass off the ground."

The fuzzy little shit resembled a hybrid between a cat and a dragon. The species name didn't have an English translation but pretty much meant *little dragon*. They were pains in the ass that some of us on this side of the veil allowed to hang around. I supposed Nika could be considered a pet, but I saw her as more of a careless roommate that never contributed or cleaned.

She eyed me curiously for a moment, tilting her furry dragon head, twitching long ears that tapered into points. The tail that swished about behind her was striped with purple and green scales, the tip a puff of black fur. Feathered wings helped her leap gracefully to the balcony floor. About as big as a medium sized dog, Nika wasn't a strong flyer, more of a glider.

Winding around my legs, she let out a croaky bark that didn't sound quite like any animal earth side. Absently I bent to scratch her behind an ear before following her back into the apartment.

The Circle of the Veil had spared no expense. My apartment was a luxury penthouse in the top of a highly sought location. Not that I got to spend much time in it. But when I did have a few minutes to myself, it was nice to have them in a place like this.

I followed Nika to the fireplace. She stared blankly at it until I snapped my fingers, igniting the flames. Then without so much as a nod of thanks, the ungrateful shit curled up on the blanket in front of the hearth and nodded off.

"Must be nice not to have a care in the world," I muttered, considering another cold shower.

Since I'd left the library and Blaze within it, I'd kicked myself endlessly. Not just for leaving her there yearning with a hunger I'd forced upon her but for letting any of it happen in the first place.

Of all the women, it had to be one under my authority. I was forbidden to touch her. Which might very well explain why I wanted to touch her so fucking much. I'd been with thousands of women. Hundreds of thousands. I'd never counted since, as an incubus, such a feat would have been futile.

My fall into darkness had come with a price. There was always a price, and thus was mine: to fuel my power from the sexual desire of my lovers while leaving them hopelessly and helplessly addicted. It proved a great way to ensure I had a steady stream of lust-charged women to meet my every need.

Every need except one. Though whether or not love was a need for my kind was arguable. How could anyone love someone who enslaved them with lust? Addicted they only craved me more with every touch.

I didn't know shit about love, but I knew that wasn't it. Turning Blaze into a lust-smitten incubus junkie would ruin everything that made her so damn tempting. And if I thought she resented me now, she would downright hate me with every fiber of her being if I let things get any worse.

Rayne had probably stepped in and fucked her raw, giving her everything I so badly wished I could. The very thought had me throwing a fist at my bedroom wall as I stormed in and slammed the door shut.

The spacious room felt like a vast and barren landscape, lacking the draw it once had. I strode past the giant bed covered in puffy black feather-filled blankets and into the attached bathroom. Cranking the water on cold, I disrobed and stepped beneath the icy spray.

A cold shower to relieve my burning desire had to be just about the stupidest fucking thing I'd ever heard. Leave it to humans to convince themselves that freezing your nether regions would quell a hunger that burned from the inside out.

Because I wasn't a fucking insipid human, I turned the tap back toward hot and fisted my cock. For the third time since I'd come home, I jerked off to Blaze. Her upper lip curved softly, and she gnawed at it when she grew frustrated. When she sassed me and knew she'd get away with it, she laughed so brightly. But mostly, I just thought about the way she'd looked at me before I left: blue eyes rife with anguish and desire, pleading for me to take her the way I wanted.

I'd never maintained a relationship with any lover long enough to grow attached. I didn't want any emotional link to someone who wanted me for my incubus touch. Blaze wasn't even my lover, and I still couldn't get her out of my head. As long as we were both at Mayhem House, there was no walking away from her. I couldn't keep my distance to cut us both off.

Why did I care about the feisty redhead who was so quick to call me on my bullshit? How the hell had she managed to get so close without me noticing? And there I was, begging her to let me get even closer like a raging idiot.

She was right not to trust me.

Getting too close would only hurt her, in more ways than one. But if I didn't find out what it felt like to be inside her pretty damn soon, I might just lose my fucking mind.

CHAPTER FIFTEEN

I'd never been to The Cat's Claw, but Tavi insisted that it was the only place in the city worth drinking at. Needing to surround myself with estrogen after the previous night's debauchery, I'd jumped on Dalyn's idea to go out for a girls' night. Tavi hadn't been quite as enthusiastic, but she grumbled something about coming along only if she could choose where we went. So here we were, listening to the raucous music from a local band called Sacred Stone and drinking in a bar that occupied the end unit of a strip mall.

Well, Dalyn and Tavi were drinking; I busied myself with taking stock of our fellow patrons. Most were early twenty-somethings drinking as much as their human bodies could consume before they vomited and blacked out. No fanged or furred types among the crowd, aside from us.

Nobody looked like a Fed either, although someone undercover wouldn't be obvious. Maybe I was paranoid. This Mayhem Task Force shit had gotten inside my head. I'd been here a month, and already I could barely recall my life before.

The nightclub itself was relatively big considering its location. More than enough space to pack in a few hundred people looking to get shitfaced. Nothing stood out as special or memorable about it. From floor to ceiling it was a drab gray. More standing room than sitting areas, apparently they didn't want anyone to get too comfortable.

"We should really do this more often." Dalyn slammed a shot glass down on the weird standing table the three of us clustered around. "A night out. Just us."

"If you say so," Tavi snarked, watching the band with a critical eye. When the waitress brought by the next round of drinks, Tavi received twice as many as Dalyn, as it had been all night so far.

Shifters could handle more alcohol than humans, but they weren't nearly as adept at processing it as Tavi seemed to think. When she reached drink number six in less than an hour, I watched her more closely. Her relaxed and unusually calm energy didn't feel right.

The full moon was two nights away. How it might affect her, I didn't know, but the way Rayne told it, the wolf's instincts and mentality were strongest during the three days when it was fullest. So strong that some shifters couldn't handle being in human form at all, let alone retain that humanity in wolf form. He said instinct had a way of taking over, which I understood in my own way.

Trying to keep the conversation flowing, I added, "It's nice to get out of that house for a while without it involving a car chase."

"The night's not over yet," Dalyn giggled drunkenly, aiming her phone to take a photo of the pink cherry-topped cocktail she'd ordered.

The bright red maraschino cherry mocked me. I could hear Nova's alluring tone when he called me cherry bomb. My loins tensed, and I consciously shoved away thoughts of Nova.

"Don't jinx us, Sabrina," I joked, nudging her elbow.

"Only Ghost gets to call me that," she protested with a laugh. Plucking the cherry from her drink, she popped it into her mouth, dropping the stem on the table. "Speaking of that sexy as fuck vampire, do you think he'd kill me if I tried to sleep with him?"

Before I could respond, Tavi beat me to it with a sly and slightly slurred, "I don't know but Blaze definitely will. He's one of her bones, you know."

Mortified, I picked up the abandoned cherry stem and twisted it between my fingers. "Tavi, what the hell?"

"Is he really?" At the first hint of juicy house gossip, Dalyn was all over it. "Are you doing Ghost too? You lucky fucking bitch. Can I be you? Just for, like, a day? No, make it a week."

Wishing I could drop off my chair and disappear under the table, I shot Tavi a pointed glare.

She smiled and downed another drink.

"Ghost was a one-night stand before we both came to the house," I explained, trying to keep it short. Girl talk was fine, but I'd rather not have my personal life be the main subject of discussion. "We've reconnected, but it's not the way Tavi makes it sound."

Tavi chuckled, loving my discomfort. "Oh, I'm sorry. I must have been mistaken by the sound of your threesome last night."

Damn keen werewolf hearing. Had Corr also heard?

"Damn, bitch, please trade me lives. For one hour. I might know a spell that could make it happen." Dalyn's loopy laughter made it hard to tell if she was joking or not.

I waved a hand to brush off the whole thing. "Give me a break. It's not nearly as exciting as Tavi makes it sound."

No, it was far more exciting than I could begin to describe, which is why I wouldn't try. Also, as much as I enjoyed my time with these ladies, I wasn't ready to open up and spill everything.

"Honestly, it sounds fucking terrible." Tavi's sour opinion wasn't entirely surprising. "That's a lot of dick to keep happy and for what? Eventually it's gonna go south, and you'll still be stuck in the house with them, if you don't die first."

"Thanks, Tav. Your positive demeanor is always appreciated, like a light on the darkest of nights. It warms my cold, undead heart." My deadpan delivery wasn't appreciated by the moody wolf, but Dalyn kept up her giggles between sips of cocktail.

Tavi wasn't all terrible. On occasion, the person inside that she tried so hard to hide slipped out. "Hey, I don't blame you for getting yours. But I swore off men the night my ex tried to rip my throat out. Hell, I swore off people." She stopped herself before she could reveal more of her history.

A strange quiet settled over the table, made more awkward by the voices and music all around us.

In an effort to lighten the mood and steer the conversation back on course, Dalyn blurted, "Well I need to get mine too. It's been at least six months since I got laid. Blaze can have every guy in the house for all I care. I want a man that doesn't know where I live."

Both Tavi and I laughed at that. I gestured to the packed nightclub. "Take your pick. I'm sure there are dozens of guys in here who'd happily service you."

"Service me," Dalyn repeated, rolling her eyes at my word choice. "I don't want to be serviced. I want to be screwed senseless. At this point any fuck could be my last. I need a man who can bring it."

We spent the next ten minutes helping Dalyn pick out potential hotties, most of which she never planned to approach. Until Tavi got it into her head that she needed to force Dalyn to take action.

"Just go talk to him. Look. He's sitting alone." Nodding toward a man who waited for his friend to return, Tavi gave Dalyn a push in his direction.

Drunk and lacking regard for how much stronger she was than the human witch, Tavi's shove sent Dalyn toppling into the group of women gathered around a table next to us. With no hope of keeping her balance in stiletto heels after being overbalanced by a careless werewolf, she fell on her ass, splashing her cocktail everywhere, including all over two of the women, almost taking one of them down with her.

I leaped up to grab Dalyn's arm, helping her back to her feet. "Are you ok?"

Before I could turn to give Tavi shit, the woman who'd almost fallen shoved Dalyn into me. What the shit? Drunk humans had stupid amounts of fearlessness.

"Watch yourself, bitch," the woman hissed at Dalyn, as if it had been her fault.

I held up a hand, prepared to explain that she wasn't at fault. No need. Tavi swooped in, stepping up to snarl into the woman's face. The irises of her glassy, bloodshot eyes slowly seeped across the whites. Shit.

"What the fuck did you just say?" Tavi's hands clenched into fists.

Couldn't make fists with claws, so good sign, right? I couldn't be sure. If she wolfed out in here, she'd be sentencing herself to certain death.

To Dalyn I said, "We have to get her out of here."

Wide eyed and somewhat sobered by the sudden turn of events, she nodded, unable to tear her gaze from the scene unfolding before us. An intoxicated werewolf days before the full moon wasn't going to come quietly.

"I said," the angry woman shouted into Tavi's face. "Watch yourself, bitch." She hit the emphasis on bitch so much harder this time.

That was all it took. Shocking us all, Tavi's fist flew. It slammed into the woman's jaw so hard she went down with limbs flailing. The woman's friends jumped into action, shouting for the bouncers and moving to help her sit up. Nose bloody, she mumbled incoherently, eyes rolling back in her head.

I grabbed Tavi's wrist, ready for it when the other fist swung my way. I blocked with my forearm. "We are leaving. Now." My tone left no room for argument. Maybe I couldn't growl or flash giant fangs, but I was stronger than her. I caught her other wrist tight, making sure she remembered it.

"Get off me, Blaze." Tavi tried to shake free, her eyes all wolf.

I let her go, and she stormed toward the exit, not as steady on her feet as a werewolf should be. Loaded. I exchanged a concerned look with Dalyn, and we followed, keeping Tavi in our sights so she couldn't lose us in the parking lot.

"Well, that escalated quickly," Dalyn breathed softly when we stepped from the noisy club into the much quieter night.

Knowing Tavi could hear us, I just pointed up at the waxing gibbous moon.

Although I was ready to chase her down if she bolted, Tavi got into the backseat of the SUV we'd arrived in without issue. When I got into the driver's seat, I noticed that her fingertips were now claws and fangs poked out from beneath her lips. Was it safe to have her at my back while I drove us home? Dalyn seemed to have the same thought. In the passenger seat, she slid a small white charm from her purse and stroked it softly.

We were almost back to the house, having driven in awkward silence aside from the radio, when Tavi said with a slur, "She had it coming and you both know it."

"That's not the point, Tav." I tried for a calm, rational tone. I wasn't arguing with a drunk wolf. "It wouldn't have happened if you hadn't shoved Dalyn. We're supposed to keep a low profile in public. Pretty sure that includes no bar fights. I mean, look at you. You almost wolfed out in there."

She couldn't argue that so she stewed in silence. When we got back to the house and I saw her stumble on the steps leading up to the front door, I made a mental note to cut Tavi off after four in the future. The wolf couldn't handle her booze this close to a full moon. Or maybe ever for all I knew.

"Come on." I put an arm around her shoulders and steered her toward the stairs once we got inside. "Let's get your annoying, drunk ass into bed."

Tavi tried to shrug me off but gave up when I proved immovable. "Shit, Blaze, your ego is out of control if you think everyone in this house wants to fuck you." Her delivery was so sincere I couldn't be sure if she was messing with me or not.

From behind us Dalyn jokingly quipped, "I don't know about that. Frankly, I'm curious what the big deal is. The guys seem to like her."

I snorted in amusement. "I question the personal standards of killers, myself included. Can't trust a single one of us."

Once we reached the top of the stairs Tavi shrugged me off and practically kicked her door open. When she tried to close it in my face, I caught it and forced my way inside.

Dalyn followed right behind me. "Tavi, what's going on with you? Are you all right?"

Tavi left the light off, so I switched it on, lowering it to a dim setting. The frustrated wolf moved about her room like a small tornado, stripping off her jacket and throwing it onto the TV set while upsetting a bedside lamp.

"Stay by the door." Pointing a clawed finger at Dalyn, Tavi flopped onto the end of the bed, long black hair falling to hide half her face. "I can't promise that I won't snap again. I feel very… wolfy."

She looked damn wolfy too. I put myself between the two of them, so Tavi would have to go through me to get to Dalyn. I racked my brain for the right thing to say.

Tavi filled in the blank spaces. Grabbing a pillow off the bed, she crushed it to her chest. "I can't control the wolf. Once it's free, it takes over. I don't even know what I'm doing. The kill that landed me in here happened because I couldn't stop it, not because I wanted to do it. That's why I don't shift unless I have to. Unfortunately, on a full moon night, I have no choice." She paused, wolf eyes drifting over us. "So there it is. The truth about why I'm here. I guess this makes us friends or some shit like that." That admission probably never would've come out without the booze.

"Of course it does, sweetie," Dalyn gushed, hands clasped like it was all she could do to keep from rushing Tavi for a hug.

"Don't ruin it by being disgustingly sweet, ok? Now get out. I want to pass out without the two of you staring at me like I'm some broken friggin' doll." Tavi threw the pillow in our direction, but it landed several feet away. She lay down on the bed and rolled over, giving us her back.

Dalyn left the room.

I started to follow, pausing in the threshold. "I know what it's like to have an ability you can't control. If you ever want to talk or—"

"Get out, Blaze."

Without another word I closed the door. Tavi hated how vulnerable the truth made her. Yet she'd shared it anyway. Maybe it had been the liquor or maybe she just needed to finally share her truth with someone else. I was glad she'd told us, that she'd reached out in her own way.

We didn't have anyone outside this house. Might as well try to have someone inside it. We were all broken here.

CHAPTER SIXTEEN

T he night of the full moon was a prime time for every supernatural but most especially for the shifters and spell casters. Although the energy of the moon left an electrical charge on the atmosphere and added a little kick to my step, it didn't move us vampy types the way it moved the others.

Which was why Ghost and I were stuck at Mayhem House on standby.

Nova had sent a message through Smudge, the watchdog team leader, who'd called me shortly after sunset. Full moon nights always drew shady FPA activity, and Nova wanted me ready to go if needed. Bastard incubus couldn't even show his face to deliver the message himself. Shocker.

The shifters on our team would be running as wolves tonight in a safe place outside the city. Tavi too, despite her flippant remarks about preferring to be locked in the interrogation room downstairs. She'd been ordered to join Rayne and Corr, both solid choices for the situation she faced. If I were in her shoes, I'd have wanted them by my side.

Dalyn and Retta holed up downstairs, working on magic stuff in the library. Ira had popped his head into the kitchen to tell them he didn't feel well and would be staying in his bedroom. Still recovering from that gunshot wound to the leg, he used it as an excuse to retreat from the rest of us and avoid as many duties as possible. He never interacted with us more than necessary, spending most of his time in his room.

Much to Dalyn's relief. She'd admitted to being wary of his spell crafting.

"Think we're going to get any action tonight?" I glanced at Ghost who shot balls around the pool table by himself while I lounged in a lazy heap on the living room couch.

He turned to me with a brow raised, a flash of fangs in his sly grin. "Baby, if you want some action, all you gotta do is ask."

"You know if we do that we'll definitely get a call to go out."
Stretching out along the couch, I propped a hand under my head,
watching him line up another shot.

Ghost sunk the eight ball, laid the cue stick down, and turned to
me with a mischievous gleam in his eyes. "So let's do it. We'll fuck,
or we'll get the hell out of this place and make shit happen. Either way
we'll have a damn good time." His brazen delivery made me laugh.

No part of me didn't want to say to hell with it. There were
certainly worse people to be stuck with and worse things to do while
we waited. I beckoned him with a finger, and he prowled across the
living room toward me, a hunter with his prey.

But I was a hunter too—

Before Ghost reached me, my phone began to buzz. Just as I'd
called it.

"See?" I snatched my phone off the coffee table. "I knew that
would happen. Hey, Smudge, what's up?"

The sweet-toned vampiress didn't piss around with small talk.
"We've got a report of a shifted werewolf cornered by some locals in a
neighborhood near the river. Try to get there before the Feds do. Do
whatever you can to chase them off without drawing more attention to
the situation. Report back as soon as you can."

As soon as I confirmed that I understood, she hung up. After
repeating our instructions to Ghost, I added, "We better get moving.
Definitely no time for other things now."

I got up off the couch, a sense of urgency driving me.

When I turned to rush out of the room, Ghost blocked my path,
undeterred by the phone call. Sliding a hand around the back of my
neck and into my hair, he kissed me. That deep, explorative kiss left
me reeling when he pulled back.

"All right." Ghost lingered, his lips barely touching mine. "We
can go now."

I had to remind myself that there was a werewolf in trouble and
dart after Ghost as he sauntered from the room. A warm glow
enveloped me in the wake of his kiss. Spending so much time in this
house did not work in favor of my willpower.

"Wanna drive?" Tossing me the keys from the table in the
foyer, Ghost held the front door open. "I like having my hands free in
case we get a tail. Unless you want to run defense."

A click and the shuffling of feet on the stairs above preceded Ira as he slowly made his way down, grumbling to himself about all the goddamn steps. With a slip of a glance in our direction, he dismissed us and entered the kitchen. I still didn't know what he'd done to get here, and I wasn't sure I wanted to.

"I'll drive." I jumped at the chance to let Ghost run defense. His skills were more fully developed and not as likely to kill us both. As far as I knew.

The sleek black Dodge Charger in the garage was new. So Nova had been taking some of our requests seriously. Yeah, I would happily drive the hell out of that monster on wheels.

I punched the address Smudge had texted into the GPS on my phone. Only about ten minutes away, that was still way too much time for a wolf cornered by people who believed it to be a real wild animal. Humans were the absolute worst. They call us the monsters, but at least we're up front about it.

The drive over was relatively uneventful. Ghost and I settled into an easy quiet, broken here and there by casual conversation that didn't feel forced or awkward. Despite the vampire's mysterious air, I felt comfortable with him. And it wasn't just because he'd had no problem blowing my mind in bed.

"That the place?" Ghost studied the abandoned gas station ahead. Muscles in his jaw flexed. "This doesn't feel right. Don't pull into the parking lot. There's only one way in and out. Actually don't stop at all. Just drive by."

Immediately my skin crawled. Nobody was around. The businesses in this area hadn't been in operation for some time, and the closest residential street was at least a few blocks away.

"Do you think it's the wrong address? Or a false call?" My money was on the latter. How well did Smudge know every one of her sources?

Obeying the speed limit, I coasted past the gas station at the address we'd been given, not a person in sight. We rounded a slight bend in the road ahead and came upon a barricade of FPA vehicles parked across the street. A second set of vehicles were lined up behind the first, making it impossible to blast through.

"Motherfucker," I swore, having no choice but to stop. "They laid a trap for us. What the hell do we do?"

As we slowed, a few more cars pulled up behind us. We were blocked in on every side. Putting the car in park, I turned off the engine but made no move to get out. Half a dozen Feds approached us, heavy guns at the ready. About ten more agents lingered behind them, crossbows raised and aimed.

Unperturbed, Ghost caught my chin gently in a hand, turning my face to his. Stroking his thumb over my jaw, he said, "We survive. We have a choice now. Fight or let them take us."

We'd been told to never let the FPA take us. Although we hadn't been specifically told it would be better for us to die first, it had been implied.

"Nova will shit a brick if we go willingly. Not to mention The Circle." Aware of the FPA agents now shouting at us to get out of the car, I reached for the door handle. I would not die in this car.

"Fuck The Circle," Ghost hissed. "It's our asses on the line. We're making this call. If you want to fight, we'll fight. But going willingly might be the easiest way to get out of this alive. Either we fight them now, or we fight them later when we break the fuck out, but there will be a fight, doll. You choose when it happens."

The image he'd painted terrified me, but with the armed men and women surrounding us, ready to rip us from the car, I had no time to choose. One thing was certain: we'd only win a fight with these odds if I bled. A lot.

While I struggled to decide, Ghost destroyed both of our phones with a surge of power, ensuring they were rendered useless if they ended up in the wrong hands. Before the Feds could get any closer, Ghost threw open his door and raised both hands. It was enough to make them stand back and see if we'd surrender. Having no choice, I got out too, holding my hands where they could be seen.

The FPA weren't worried about any weapons we might have. It was our magic they feared.

"On your knees. Now," a burly Fed with a heavy beard barked. "Or I put a bolt in your heart."

Crossbow bolts proved efficient for killing vampires. Straight up bullets hurt like hell but didn't kill us. The old stake through the heart thing was pretty much true. Thick, long, and deadly, the Feds had come packing. No tranquilizers this time.

Ghost eased around the front of the car, so I was in his sight, and went to his knees as instructed. He slid me a look, a brow raised in question. He wanted to play this the smart way. I could see it in his dark eyes. The Circle of the Veil would kill us if they learned we didn't even put up a fight.

But a fight meant death. That was promised by the faces of all the agents present. Hard, angry expressions, fingers on triggers, my demise surrounded me on every side.

Bleed now or surrender. I had no other choices and only a second to decide.

I could create a gash with a fang, let the blood run out. Blow them all away. Somewhere deep within, I desperately wanted to. The urge was so sinister and unwelcome that it left a bitter taste in my mouth, making me recoil. I couldn't do it. I didn't have the control, and I suspected that the part of me where the blood magic dwelled didn't want me to master it.

"Any sudden moves and you die." Another agent barked.

When neither of us made any effort to fight, we were each surrounded by Feds who pinned us face first to the ground while securing our hands behind our backs. The sound of so many heartbeats reverberated loud in my head. Panic rose up as the first cuff was slapped on my wrist.

When Nova had wanted me to try this during an interrogation exercise, I'd almost lost my shit. It hadn't been my finest moment. Of course this was exactly why he'd wanted to cuff me. To prepare me in any way possible.

Still nothing could replicate the real thing.

I expected the panic to grip me now, as it had then and every time Remington had forced me into submission using any means at hand. To fight back the rising fear, I searched for Ghost, catching a glimpse of him through a cluster of FPA bodies. He didn't fight. Just like when Nova wanted to cuff him, Ghost allowed it. Welcomed it even.

Feeling my frantic stare, he met and held my gaze. How he could be so calm in the face of such uncertainty?

Sucking in a deep breath, I followed Ghost's lead. I trusted him to know how to keep us alive. Despite the well of rising alarm choking me, I let them slap cuffs on both wrists, dampening my power. We might have stood a chance if we'd opted to fight, but the odds had been stacked against us. Still, as the Feds roughly jerked us up and threw us into an armored car, I couldn't help but wonder if we would make it out. Would Nova come for us? Or leave us to whatever fate the FPA had in store?

CHAPTER SEVENTEEN

Crammed into the large boxy vehicle with FPA agents on each side of us, I stared straight ahead, acknowledging nobody. Aside from uttering threats to remind us not to try anything— not that I could—they didn't talk to us either.

Next to me, Ghost pressed his thigh against mine, reassuring me more in that subtle touch than in anything he could have said. I didn't so much as glance his way. Needing to stay focused, I stared at the hard metal wall opposite me, ignoring the Feds who sat there with weapons ready.

This was fucked.

In my head I did the alphabet backward to keep from thinking about the handcuffs holding me. They might contain my blood magic or fire it right back at me, so why was I so tempted to find out if they could?

By the time I finally managed to get through the entire alphabet without making a mistake due to nerves, we were pulling up to the abandoned hospital the FPA used as their base. Rumor had it that the hospital was haunted as hell, abandoned for good reason. Stories surrounding the place included the torments of patients and their lingering, pissed off ghosts.

Yet none of that bothered me nearly as much as the living humans with their weapons and poor decision-making skills. If any of them were smart, they'd be anywhere else right now. Although perhaps that could be said of Ghost and me as well.

The van backed up to a side door and stopped. We were roughly jerked out by too many people grabbing for us at once. Gritting my teeth, I willed myself to rein in my temper. The panic wasn't the only thing that set me off; the Feds I'd baited for Nova found that out the hard way.

If these people found out I was responsible for that, I was as good as dead. Or worse.

The hospital building was in rough shape, not only on the outside but the inside too. Ghost was tugged along ahead of me by four gun-toting agents with two following. I was shoved along behind him, given the same security. They weren't taking any chances.

We entered into a dimly lit atrium that smelled of must and a decade old layer of dirt. One set of stairs led to the upper floors, and a stairwell went down to the basement. We didn't take either set.

Instead Ghost and I were dragged into a caged elevator. It took us down.

Underground didn't feel like a good thing. Now I met Ghost's pensive gaze, searching him for any sign that he felt we should do something to stop them from taking us further. He merely winked before turning his attention to the elevator door and whatever it might reveal when it opened.

A hallway lit with retina-searing fluorescent lights ushered us into a maze of creepy FPA wonders. As we were jostled along, I noted the layout of the halls and which way we turned at each intersection. A building this large required several stairwells to get up and down. Or out.

We had to get the fuck out.

As the agents pushed us down one bright hall and then another, I tried to make note of everything I saw. We passed a closed off room that stank of chemicals and fear, a lab of some kind.

Dear God.

My relief that we hadn't gone in there proved short lived. The next hall we turned down, forced along by barked commands to move faster, was filled with cells. Prison cells. They didn't let me close enough to look through the small barred windows in the heavy metal doors. Maybe I couldn't see any occupants, but I could feel them. A few vampires lurked inside, their energies despondent. An anguished howl broke out at the end of the hall, so at least one werewolf.

My body crawled with unease. That familiar panic threatened to rise.

The ghost of a crying woman drifted out of the wall in front of us. She never seemed to notice our large group trudging toward her, though her presence added to my anxiety. Weeping softly, she disappeared into the wall on the opposite side.

I sensed great unrest here, but there was something else too. Beyond the building and its sad, dead occupants, the land beneath us thrummed with something dark and deep. Otherworldly. I felt it sniffing at me, like a dog sticking its face right in my crotch. It didn't try to communicate with me even though I got the feeling it could if it wanted to. With Feds dragging me down the hall toward God knew what, I couldn't exactly initiate a conversation with this… thing. Whatever it was, it wasn't my problem. Not right in the moment.

Then it slipped away as fast as I'd felt it.

Ghost cocked his head, like he sensed it now.

We rounded another bend and entered what I quickly identified as an interrogation room, a large one made to accommodate several people at once. Immediately fear gripped me, and I dug in my heels. Several steel chairs filled the room, all of them complete with heavy duty shackles. A tray littered with torture implements stood off to one side, gleaming wickedly beneath the green-tinted artificial lights.

"Now you want to start fighting?" The woman gripping my arm laughed. "I'd save your energy if I were you. You're going to need it."

"Unless of course," a man on my other side chimed in, "you just start talking. Tell us everything you think we want to know. Act civil, and we'll treat you that way. Act like a monster… Well, same deal."

Ghost surprised all of us by saying, "What do you want to know? I mean, make it worth our while, and maybe we can work something out here."

My jaw dropped. Was he really going rogue here or was this just a game to him? If he had something in mind for this situation, he hadn't shared it with me.

They stopped short of shoving us into the chairs. No doubt I would not be allowing anyone to force me into one of those things. The cuffs were the extent of my ability to cope right now. Shackled to a chair and tortured for information about a secret supernatural society that I didn't even ask to be part of? Hell no.

"Who do you work for?" The burly, bearded guy towered over Ghost, trying to intimidate with his size, because that's really all he had to work with.

Unfazed by the agent getting in his face, Ghost gave a lazy shake of his head. "We don't work for anyone. See, that implies that we're here willingly. But we didn't volunteer for this shit."

What in the flying crap was Ghost doing here?

The Feds didn't believe him. They turned to me for confirmation. "We don't work for anyone," I heard myself say, spewing shit at random. "In fact, we were minding our own fucking business harming absolutely no one. What's your reason for bringing us in?"

"You're a vampire. That's all the reason I need." Beardo nodded toward the tray of bloody tools. "We've got a guy who's really handy with those things. Unless you'd like to meet him, I suggest you start giving me something."

Walking the fine line between fear and rage, I waited to see how Ghost wanted to do this. He'd thrown me a curve already. In the back of my mind, I just kept asking myself how they'd known our location so precisely? How had they known we were out there at all?

For a heartbeat of a second I wondered if Ghost had just led me into a trap. Maybe he was some FPA mole planted at Mayhem House. Maybe he was just as bad as Nova, luring me into a dangerous situation to feel out my powers.

Not a single part of me believed that. First, Ghost didn't strike me as the type. Also he'd fought by my side when we intercepted the prisoner transfer. He'd stayed behind to get me on my feet when the dust cleared, despite it being a risk to himself. Something was definitely amiss at Mayhem House, but it wasn't Ghost.

He slipped a tiny wry grin my way.

Beardo didn't miss that. Brow furrowed in deep lines, his hand strayed to the stun gun on his hip. It was tough to peg his age with the beard, but I'd put him at late thirties to early forties. Like everyone else present, he had a hero complex. He really thought we were the bad guys.

"What do you want from us, man?" Ghost sounded annoyed, not at all afraid. "Seeing as you knew just how to find us, I'd say you already know what you want us to tell you. Or at least, you think you do."

"That so?" Beardo pulled the stun gun from his belt and twirled it in one hand. Nodding to his peers, he barked, "Put them in the chairs."

This had gone too far already, and we'd only been here a few minutes. We never should have let them bring us inside. How were our odds any better in here? We had a few less agents surrounding us since entering the ramshackle building but still a dozen or more.

My hold on the calm, controlled front I forced was slipping. If they put me in a chair, if they did things—

No, that would not be happening. Even if I had to kill every person in this room, I would not face torture at the hands of these government scum.

Their world was not ours. Considering they did a shit job of handling human affairs, it astounded me that they believed they had a right to get involved in ours. We had The Circle of the Veil policing our every move, and that was more than enough.

Jerked toward the closest chair I couldn't do much with my arms trapped behind me, but panic didn't give a shit about that. It went wild. No thought, just instinct. Using fangs, I bit into my bottom lip, spilling enough blood to fill my mouth. If the power ricocheted back at me, I'd have achieved nothing other than making myself look like an idiot. Of course rational thought didn't factor into moments of fight or flight, even if the reward outweighed the risk.

My blood magic bubbled up, blasting through my body, seeking a way out. The power found the barrier in the cuffs around my wrists and blasted right through it, obliterating their magic wards.

After that it was nothing to snap the cuffs off completely.

Rounding on the shocked agents, I threw both hands up, using a telekinetic push to fling them away. They flew in various directions, crashing into each other and overturning the equipment tray.

Wisely Ghost started for the door, hands still cuffed behind him. I followed hot on his heels. If we were lucky enough to get a head start, agents could still swarm us in mere seconds.

"This way." Turning right as we left the room, Ghost darted down the hall, then veered left down another. We moved much faster than the humans scrambling in chase, but they'd certainly already called for backup.

After turning down another hall that ended in a morgue of all damn things, we ducked into a utility closet. Ghost turned to hold his wrists out to me. "Care to work some of that badass magic and get these things off me?"

"What? I can't. I mean, I don't know how I did that. I panicked." Despite my lack of confidence, I reached for the cuffs binding his wrists.

"You think you're a mess, Blaze, but what you have is unique, something nobody else has. You've gotta stop fearing it and start using it. Come on. You can do this." Lowering his voice as the sound of shouts drew closer, he said, "We can't be here when the sun rises. The more time passes, the less chance we have of leaving by then."

Using the tip of a fang, I pricked a small hole in the tip of finger, wary of letting too much blood flow. Then I grabbed the cuffs holding Ghost bound, and with another splash of blood magic, broke the spell on them. The lock clicked, and Ghost slipped the cuffs from his wrists, dropping them to the floor.

A slight wave of dizziness hit, and I had to grab hold of the wall to steady myself.

Ghost gripped my shoulder, turning me to face him. "We are getting out of here. Mark my words, baby girl. But a lot of that is going to count on you. I'm gonna need you to really bring it. You've got this, ok?"

I had to get out without losing my entire shit. We were trapped inside a large scary old building filled with nutjob humans who didn't want us to leave. The ghosts and the strange spirit that dwelled here didn't even register on my radar. They weren't the threat here.

"Ok." I nodded vigorously, finding myself encouraged by the calm in his dark eyes. "Just promise me that when things get ugly, you won't let me hurt you."

CHAPTER EIGHTEEN

GHOST

Looking back on the night I first met Blaze, I didn't doubt for a moment that it was kismet. Even though we'd gone our separate ways after our back-alley encounter, I knew I would see her again. This wild beauty held a secret in her blood, a power like nothing I'd encountered.

"Don't worry about me. I'm just a ghost, remember?" Seeing the fear in her enchanting blues recede, I treated myself to a handful of her ass as I nudged her toward the closet door. The sound of voices coming in our direction cut off. They'd turned another way. "It's now or never."

Gripping the doorknob tight, Blaze turned it slowly, edging it open. Maybe we shouldn't have surrendered and come willingly. Surrounded as we'd been, I'd gone with my gut and raised my hands. My gut had never failed me yet.

The thing about haunted buildings, especially those with as much unrest as this place, they had a way of drawing the attention of bigger, darker entities. Such as the one that dwelled within the land. I could feel it lurking like a shark swimming beneath our boat, ready to rock us over at any time, should it so choose.

It felt demonic in origin, like it didn't belong here, on this plane. Even though I sensed that it had the power to really fuck with us, it didn't. Did the human Feds have any idea it was even here, lurking below them?

Blaze and I moved down the hall, fast but silent. The place was a goddamn maze of intersecting halls and rooms. Shouts echoed, sounding closer than they were, making it hard to judge our pursuers' location.

We were running blind, trying to find a way out that didn't include going back to the elevator they'd brought us down in. One thing I'd learned about places like this: there was always another way out.

"They've got to have a procedure in place for when prisoners break free." Blaze sounded calm, but her energy held a frantic edge.

She didn't do so well with being at anyone's mercy, even in a training exercise. Rather than playing it cool, she exploded in a fit of power that was fucking beautiful to behold. If she could just learn to rein it in and hold it until the right time, unleashing it on whomever and whatever she chose, she'd easily be the most powerful person on our team.

"We have our own protocol," I reminded her. "Survive at all costs. Even if it means leveling this entire shithole."

Blaze met my gaze and I grinned. The lady was too tightly wound. With a shake of her crimson tresses, she said, "You're fucking crazy, you know that?"

She was far from the first person to call me that, just the latest of at least a thousand women who'd uttered those words. "Loco like you wouldn't believe," I muttered more to myself than to her.

I eyed the path to our right. Something pulled me in that direction. The darkness beneath us wanted to show us the way out. I wasn't sure how I knew, but I'd take any help I could get.

"Are you talking to yourself?"

"Never mind. We've gotta move." Holding tight to her, I let the force below lead us, a risky move seeing as evil things don't do a damn thing for anyone without motive. I had no choice but to trust it. And to trust Blaze.

As we turned another bend a staircase came into view. Our exit. Just as we started to run up the stairs, a flood of agents rushed down toward us. Pulling Blaze along with me, I backed down the stairs, keeping an eye on those coming at us.

"Ghost." The tremor in her soft voice had me whirling to find another team approaching from behind. There was nowhere to retreat.

"Get on the floor. You only get one chance to obey. Now!" The shout came from one of the many gun-wielding maniacs.

Pulling Blaze against me, I surrounded us with a shimmering energy circle, a barrier that might or might not hold if they all opened fire. With her back to my chest, I made sure the crew at the bottom of the stairs could see her frightened face. Baring fangs, I drew her hair back to expose her gorgeous neck.

"If this woman bleeds, you'll all die." Seeking and finding the hard stare of the man leading the bunch, I made sure he knew that I meant business. "Think I'm kidding? There's magic in her blood wild enough to blow this shit factory apart. If you don't let us leave, I'll bleed her and take you all with us. Try me."

Next to the man who'd shouted the order, a woman leaned in close to whisper, "Agent O'Brien would never agree to killing them."

Agent O'Brien was the sister of the city's vampire queen, Alexa, a vaewolf technically, who also happened to be Circle of the Veil elite. O'Brien was the one agent we'd been told explicitly not to harm. But she was a werewolf and this was a moon night. She wasn't here to step in on our behalf.

Dude calling the shots used that to his advantage. "Yeah, well do you see her anywhere? Fuck it. Fuck this asshole."

One factor they'd failed to consider was how surrounding us in a hallway with only stairs at the end came with the risk of potentially hitting a fellow agent. He took the shot without warning, but I expected it. I had faith in my circle, and it held. The crossbow bolt hit the side and fell harmlessly to the floor. The next shot he took ricocheted off the barrier, toward the group of agents gathered behind us. Shouts rang out as people ducked and covered.

"This is all you, gorgeous," I murmured in Blaze's ear, loving the way she trembled against me.

"Make me bleed," she said, voice strong, angry even. "Do it now."

Not needing further encouragement, I bit into the pulse in her neck. Blood filled my mouth, tangy but sweet. Powerful. It teased my cock to life. The magic in her blood almost threw me on my ass. I hit the side of the barrier, losing my hold on it. The entire thing came down.

Hands held before her, Blaze conducted the powerful force, turning in a circle to spread the blast. An explosion of wild magic, it went off like a battery of fireworks, scattering in every direction. It hit the Feds much like it had the last time I'd witnessed her at work, tearing through them like they were paper dolls.

From far beneath us I could feel the entity in the earth watching closely. Enjoying the havoc we wreaked, it urged us on.

Bodies dropped, blood leaking from various orifices. Agents tried to flee. Shots were taken and quickly turned back on the shooter. Blaze's magic, once released, seemed to know what to do. It knew what made her feel threatened, and it took aim. Red light filled her hands, darting in several directions. Brow furrowed in concentration, blood dripping down the side of her neck in two thin lines, Blaze obliterated the Feds like a fucking goddess.

As the bleeding slowed, the power subsided. Blaze stumbled toward me, shaking her head. I had no trouble dealing with the agents left standing. A few well-aimed psi balls took them down. Fangs in an artery took them out.

Once the stairs were clear, I grabbed Blaze and pushed her on ahead of me. I'd seen how the blood magic weakened her, so my bite had been precise. Just a spill, not a flood.

We made it up the stairs to the ground level to find a locked and alarmed security door. Using both hands, palms extended, I hit it with a blast that disabled the alarm and broke the lock. It took more exertion than expected, but the door flew open and we were out.

Hand in hand we ran across the grassy expanse of land the hospital sat on to the street beyond. Since neither of us had a phone, we had to get to a busy public place where we could call for a ride.

Avoiding the light in all its forms as we fled the FPA facility, we became the shadows, something I'd gotten relatively good at over the years. Living several lives enabled one to perfect such skills. Having been a so-called rogue in every one of them helped.

We emerged onto a busy street and finally came to a stop at a streetlight. Waiting to cross, Blaze turned to me with a sparkle in her eyes. "Think we lost them?"

Using her power awakened something in her, something she'd gotten used to suppressing when she should've been setting it free. It made her feel alive despite how it exhausted her. The satiated expression she wore was no lie.

"Yeah, we're good. Let's find a phone and call Smudge for a ride." I pulled Blaze's hair over the side of her neck to hide my bite. Not much caused me hesitation, but the question I wanted to ask did. "Why me, *muñeca*?" I asked, calling her doll in Spanish. "Why did you trust me to make you bleed?"

Her gaze darted over my face before focusing on the traffic light, which hadn't changed. She didn't look at me when she said, "Because I don't trust myself."

CHAPTER NINETEEN

L et's go over this again. You were on your way to the address
Smudge gave you, and the FPA surrounded you on every side.
Tell me the rest." Hands flat on the dining room table, Nova
snarled at Ghost and me. He'd been in a real mood since arriving,
shortly after sunset the night following our FPA encounter.

The three of us were in the dining room. Ghost sat on one side
of the long table. I sat across from him, width wise, while Nova
bitched and paced around the room.

"How many more times are you going to make us repeat this
story? I'm hungry. I need to get out of here." Slumping back in my
chair, I mimed eating off the empty plate in front of me. Anything to
hurry this interrogation along. Because that's what it felt like.

The night before, Ghost and I had made it back to the house
without further incident. Although I'd have liked to lay low for a night
or two after a scare like that, I needed blood. Taking from Rayne was
an option, but shifter blood became a risk in great quantities or
frequent repetition. Already I found myself homing in on his heartbeat
the moment he walked in the room.

"You talk until I can find what I need to prove to The Circle
that you don't deserve to die for last night's arrest." In a sudden flare
of temper, Nova shoved away from the table, upsetting a chair in the
process. "Not only do they find it suspicious that the Feds knew
exactly where you'd be, they question why you'd willingly let them
take you. They're convinced that you only got out so easily because
you struck a deal or you already work for them."

I stared at Nova aghast. Across from me, Ghost chuckled,
amused by this turn of events. As much as I would've loved to laugh
this off, I couldn't find the humor in the accusation.

"What the fuck?" Baffled by The Circle's reasoning, I fumbled
to defend myself. "Why would we set up a fake arrest, Nova? Do you
seriously think any of that shit is true? We told you how we got out."

"Of course I don't think any of its true, but if they think you're
a risk, they won't take the chance." Kicking the toppled chair out of
his way, Nova's wings flared, a sign of his annoyance. "If I tell them

how you escaped, they'll know about your blood magic, and unfortunately the FPA already does. Exactly what I'd hoped to keep from both of them."

Arms crossed, Ghost leaned back in his chair, the epitome of cool. Nothing about this fazed him. If anything, he'd enjoyed our little adventure last night. "Instead of finding reasons to kill the two strongest people on this team, maybe The Circle should be more concerned with how the Feds knew where to find us."

Nova shot a glare at Ghost, like he was offended the vampire had dared to speak. Since catching a glimpse of the almost-healed bite mark on my neck, Nova had been extra snarly. If this were jealousy it didn't suit him.

"They already think there's a spy in the house, and right now the blame is being pinned on the two of you. The wolves were all running wild outside of town, totally accounted for. The witches were here. Any other ideas?" Exasperated, Nova shoved a hand through his long, loose hair, fisting a handful before releasing it with a huff.

It shouldn't have had such a deep effect to watch him do that, but it sent a shock of desire slithering down to my nether regions. I couldn't help but remember being wrapped around him in the library, all but begging him to fuck me. Ghost's presence took my mind down a filthy three-way path.

"Could be someone on the watchdog team," Ghost offered. "Many of them know where we're being sent."

His smoky voice shook me out of the fantasy while also making me want it more. Seriously? My life was literally on the line, and all I could think about with Nova in the room was screwing these guys senseless. The incubus temptation was a powerful foe, insistent on testing my will.

"It's possible," Nova agreed grudgingly. "I'll look into it. Keep in mind that, to The Circle, you are both expendable unless you prove why the hell you shouldn't be. Neither of you have reached that point."

We'd seen nothing inside the FPA base that The Circle didn't already know about from others who'd been inside. Maybe if we'd brought them something new, they would've been willing to go easier on us.

"What are we supposed to do?" Concern for my survival pushed back the incubus heat. "It's not like we can prove ourselves."

Nova didn't appear any happier about this than I was. His wings ruffled and stretched before settling behind him. "I'll see what I can do to keep them from making any sudden decisions. If I can convince them there's a spy on the watchdog team, they might hold off. If not…" His crimson gaze darted to Ghost. "Do you mind giving us a moment alone?"

What the hell? I wanted to shout at Ghost to stay but instead sat there in awkward silence as he exited the room without a sound or a glance back. Being alone with Nova was risky, but surely the dining room in a house filled with people would keep things clothed.

Once Nova was sure that nobody lingered within earshot, he turned to me. "Is there anything you'd like to say about last night now that it's just the two of us?"

I saw where he steered this conversation and refused to play the role he hoped I'd play. "Are you asking me if I want to turn on Ghost to save my own ass?"

Because no demon knew shame for their evil, Nova merely shrugged, unapologetic. "Maybe I am."

Was this a test? Because it felt like a test.

"Do you really think I'd do that? Sell out someone else to save myself? If you think that's who I am, Nova, then you haven't been paying attention to anything other than what's between my legs." My temper flared, and I shoved my chair back as I stood up. I didn't let it hit the floor as Nova had, catching it with a hand before it could tip over.

Yeah, I was mad now, ready to clock him for having the nerve to suggest that I'd betray Ghost or anyone else in this house. Remaining where I was beside the table, I braced myself when he came toward me.

He stopped on the other side, keeping the table between us. Still too close. "That's not at all who I think you are." His calm response didn't match the white knuckled way he gripped the back of a chair. "But it sure as fuck would make this a lot easier."

"Sorry to disappoint you."

"I'm not disappointed, Blaze. I'm fucking frustrated." Nova pulled the chair out and sat down, looking defeated and vicious. "The only way I can see out of this is to tell them the truth about your blood magic. Most people in this city don't have power like that. Those who do either end up Circle elite or dead."

"Why do you say that like being elite is just as bad as being dead?" I asked, afraid of the answer.

Nova studied me, like maybe he wasn't sure how candid to be. "For some people, it is. Others, not so much. But it means always being under their thumb, at their beck and call. Always providing something they can't get from anyone else. That's what keeps you around as Circle elite. You're too good for that shit, cherry bomb."

"But not too good for this?" Clenching my hands into tight fists, I made no effort to hide my anger. "To be used as bait. Kept as an expendable killer with an expiry date. Then blamed the first time something goes wrong. Don't expect me to pity you for being poor, hard done by, Circle of the fucking Veil elite. And don't you dare ever ask me to sell out someone in this house again." Done with Nova and his Circle bullshit, I stormed from the room.

He was already waiting for me in the kitchen. Damn his ability to do that shit. "Don't get all holier than thou on me," he growled, baring beastly fangs. His serpentine tail whipped about angrily behind him. "I don't make the rules, but I sure as fuck have been breaking them. For you."

The demon was stressed. I got that. We all were. I moved to put the kitchen island between us but listened as he continued.

"I should've reported your blood magic to them as soon as I discovered it. But I didn't. Instead I tried to help you control it so that, by the time they found out, it would only be an asset, not a risk." Emotion drove Nova to share more than I suspected he would have otherwise. "I'd sell out every person in this house before I'd lose you to those vultures. But that's what makes you better than me. And fuck if that doesn't make it so much harder."

His admission felt like a splash of cold water in my face. He really did want to protect me, but he could only do so much. My anger faded. How could I be pissed when Nova had just confessed, in his own way, to have feelings for me.

"So much for not getting attached, huh?" A wan smile made it to my lips. We'd all known the risks of getting too close.

"I'd say you have it worse than me. I'm only attached to you." Crossing his arms, Nova propped his elbows on the island and leaned toward me. "Look, it's not my place to say shit about who else you spend time with, but throw me a bone here, Blaze. Am I just kidding myself? Is this thing between us one sided?" To really make his question hit home, Nova shielded, actively cloaking his erotic vibes, reining it in so it didn't flow freely around him. So it couldn't influence my answer.

Talk about being put on the spot. It was a fair question though. I liked Nova. Really, I did. But he was a demon. He was my superior and he had orders to obey. I couldn't trust him. All the fireworks he managed to set off between my legs wouldn't change that.

"It's not one sided," I said truthfully, tapping my fingernails on the countertop. "But it's not as simple as saying there's something between us either."

"Of course not. Nor should it be. There's nothing simple about you, firecracker." Pushing away from the counter, Nova spread his wings, filling the kitchen with the mass of black feathers. "For the record, I'd still go to bat for you even if you felt nothing for me at all. I don't want you to think everything I do is for my own gain."

The incubus demon cared what I thought of him? How incredibly endearing. It was perhaps the only vulnerability he'd ever shown me.

"Don't worry, dark star. I don't think you're a total piece of crap." My lips quirked in a teasing grin. "Hey, what do you know about the spirit at the FPA base? The big one down below."

Maybe it was just me but he appeared to actually blush at the use of my stupid nickname for him. Novas were bright stars but this one was all dark. And I kind of liked him that way.

Hiding his smile, Nova said, "It's the heart of an empire that once belonged to a demon queen but now belongs to the vampire queen. It used to be deadly to vampires, so be glad it's no longer without a proper keeper. Now go take care of your vampire business, and I'll catch up with you later tonight."

I rolled my eyes, although vampire business wasn't entirely wrong. When taking from willing victims, it did tend to be a formal transaction of sorts.

"Where are you going?" Not that I expected him to tell me, but it didn't hurt to ask since I knew it had something to do with me.

"I'm going to do whatever I can to keep the heat off you and Ghost. Can't make any promises. Wish me luck. If you believe in that kind of thing." With that, Nova was gone. The air moved in response to his exit, like a heavy current rippled through.

To the empty place where he'd just stood, I whispered, "Good luck."

CHAPTER TWENTY

NOVA

As soon as I left Blaze, I went straight to the location I'd been given. The address here in the city didn't surprise me. Anyone sent by The Circle of the Veil powers that be to speak on their behalf always chose a meeting spot that couldn't be traced back to where they'd come from or to those who sent them. The identities of those at the very highest places of power were unknown to all except those who worked closest with them. Everyone else, myself included, received instruction from a handler.

Before I walked in the door of the upscale downtown piano bar, I snapped my fingers, clothing myself in the expected attire for the place. I wasn't much of a suit guy, but I'd learned to play many roles for The Circle.

Hands shoved in my pockets, I ambled up to the table where Kylo sat sipping wine like he was some kind of goddamn connoisseur. Holding his glass out, he used it to motion for me to take the seat across from him at the tiny round table. Kylo, like me, was an immortal. The Circle had been sending him to deliver messages and speak on their behalf long before they created the team at Mayhem House. Dressed in quality threads from the other side, he looked like he should've been attending a party at a castle rather than slumming at a high-end jazz bar. His dark-brown skin made his teal eyes gleam especially bright in the dimly lit room. He watched me sit down, looking smug as fuck.

The thing about Kylo that made him especially unbearable was, though he was immortal, he was no demon. This jerk was an angel.

Naturally he'd chosen a table near the back where he could watch the entire room. It was littered with people in fancy dress, out for a night of forced fronts. A stage near the front housing a baby grand piano was currently occupied by a woman crooning about a man who'd done her wrong. Humans. So pitifully tied to their emotions that they'd give the power to manipulate them to another.

"Nova, nice of you to arrive on time. For once." Leave it to Kylo to open with an insult. He gestured to the glass of wine in front of me. "I took the liberty of ordering for you. I hope that's all right. You strike me as a red kind of guy."

So he wanted to play it shallow and barbed, did he? Knowing he wanted to bait me made it easier to pick up the glass with a nod of thanks and take a drink without giving him the reaction he sought.

"There's no spy on my team," I declared, getting right to it. "I suggest you doublecheck everyone on the watchdog team."

Kylo swirled the wine in his glass while staring at me intently over the rim. "Not possible. The watchdog team is heavily vetted. If there's a spy, it's in that house. What makes you so sure it's not the two vampires?"

Tasting the wine, it immediately soured in my mouth. I forced myself to swallow. "It's not them. They were jumped by the Feds because someone gave their location away. Why should they be held responsible for that?"

"They went willingly. Why wouldn't they have put up a fight?" Kylo finished his wine and reached for the bottle of white next to the bottle of red in the middle of the table. Pretentious bastard.

"Because they were outnumbered. They chose to play it safe and wait for an opportunity to escape. As soon as they got one, they took it." My tone was light but clipped. I'd known the powers that be were going to be cunts about this.

"And what opportunity was that?" he countered, taking great joy in his job. And who could blame him? I'd have enjoyed it too. When I didn't answer fast enough, he added, "It benefits nobody if you lie, least of all your vampires."

A demon did his best work when he could deliver a total truth and still have it work out to his advantage. I didn't feel that this was one of those situations. Knowing Kylo would go ahead and label Blaze and Ghost spies, I had no choice but to be honest.

"One of them has power in the blood. Once shed, it sets off a violent reaction. Incredibly powerful and most definitely useful. But due to the sensitive nature of the magic, it can only be used in dire circumstances." Inwardly I groaned at my effort to paint Blaze's magic in a light that showed it as an asset for our cause. Who was I trying to convince here?

"Which one? Let me guess. It's the woman with the sinfully red hair. Seems exactly your type. Have you bedded her yet? No, don't tell me. It's more fun to guess." Kylo chuckled wickedly into his wine glass. "So what I'm hearing is that she's a loose cannon and you didn't want us to know about it."

I'd learned long ago that it wasn't worth the energy it took to argue with Kylo. As much as I'd have loved to smash a wine bottle across his face and slice him open with the shards, I knew the punishment for doing so would include at least six months of torture on the other side.

"Yeah, I guess that is what you'd hear. But that's because you don't fucking listen. She's powerful. Rare. She's not like most vampires." My delivery lacked venom but it rang with condescension. Anyone who overlooked Blaze's capabilities was a fucking idiot.

Knowing he had me on the ropes, Kylo pushed me a little further, testing my patience. "What makes her different from any other blood-sucking killer? If it were up to me, we'd eliminate every last one of them."

"Do you forget that they were human once? Or do you just not care?" Poking holes in his superior façade, I shoved my wine away, losing interest in playing along.

"Of course I care," Kylo huffed like I'd insulted his haircut, which was a carefully close-cropped swath of dark curls. "Killing them would set them free from their murderous ways. Maybe then they would finally know peace."

A fucked-up way of thinking in my opinion, but that wasn't the point here. "You can't talk about every vampire as if they're the same. What about Alexa? Nobody ever expected that scrappy little vaewolf to end up where she has. A powerful queen in this city and someone whom The Circle has kept alive despite many transgressions on her part. I can't claim that Blaze is as powerful as Alexa, but she's valuable and she deserves a fair chance."

Rules could be bent and broken to protect the elite when in The Circle's best interests, but a rogue was sentenced and executed without so much as a word said in their defense. In some cases it was so open and shut, no defense would have worked. But Blaze, and even Ghost, deserved a fair shake. Nobody else could speak for them but me.

"Lucky for you, Nova, I don't make the rules. I'm just the messenger. A job that does have its perks most days. Not every day." Taking his time, Kylo sipped the wine slowly, like he savored each drop. "So here's what we're prepared to do. You will be punished for knowing about your vampire's magic and keeping it to yourself. However, your vampire will be the one to carry out said punishment."

"What the fuck are you talking about?" I snapped, no longer keeping a leash on my attitude. "If you want to punish me, go for it—take your best shot—but leave her out of it."

Feigning innocence, Kylo poured the last of his wine into his glass, making short work of the bottle. "If you want to prove there's no spy on your team, send her back into the FPA base to get proof. If they've infiltrated any of our people anywhere, there will be records. Get the proof and she lives. If her magic is so special, as you claim, she should have no problem getting out again."

The asshole knew how many of my nerves he worked. All of them. We both knew I couldn't do a damn thing about it.

With great difficulty I kept my glamour in place and did not bare fangs in his smirking face. I'd kept two details from Kylo. I hadn't shared that Blaze's aura was red nor had I shared my own personal theory on that matter. Not that I'd ever breathe a word of it to anyone.

Taking what I could only consider a win as far as The Circle of the Veil was concerned, I clenched my teeth and fists. "Fine. She'll get your damn proof."

Kylo finished off every last drop of the white wine before standing up. "I'm sure I don't have to remind you that you're not allowed to help her."

"Sure, whatever you say."

"You don't mind grabbing the bill, do you? Oh and, Nova, if your vampire is a loose cannon, I suggest you get that under control before we're here having another unpleasant conversation." With a quirk of his brows, Kylo sauntered out of the bar with a kick in his step.

One might ask what kind of angel derived such enjoyment from handing out punishments to undeserving people? Most angels were the stalwart guardian warriors people imagined them to be.

Some, however, were simply demons too chickenshit to take the fall.

CHAPTER TWENTY-ONE

The taste of fresh blood in my mouth should have perked up my mood. But the sense of dread coiling like a snake in my gut only grew.

A trip to The Wicked Kiss, the vampire bar downtown, helped take the edge off my bloodlust. Unfortunately, it wasn't enough. It had been too long since I'd hunted for the kill. Vampires could make do with willing victims, taking just enough to get by for a while, but at our core we were killers, and that need eventually had to be satisfied.

Killing anyone right now, even the worst piece of human scum, was too risky. The Circle of the Veil already had a target on my back. I wouldn't give them more to use against me.

I'd played it so damn safe that I hadn't taken more than a nip from the young woman who'd volunteered her wrist to me. She'd rambled animatedly, nervous and excited, about how it was her first time but she wanted to pop her vampire cherry – her words not mine – with someone safe like me before trying to get cozy with one of the incubus vampires who frequented the place. I was too distracted by my own problems to be insulted.

Music greeted me the moment I exited the elevator. The Wicked Kiss had recently moved into a former hotel. Bigger than the previous location, it boasted a nightclub, gambling parlor, and suites available for private feedings and whatever else people agreed to exchange behind closed doors.

As I strolled out, through the large, spacious lobby, winding my way around those waiting to get into the nightclub, I had just one thing on my mind: getting back to the house and into a hot bath. The Circle could bring the hammer down anytime. Until I knew what my fate would be, I planned to lay low and do whatever I could to avoid drawing further attention to myself.

I smacked straight into the hard chest of the man that appeared right in front of me and rebounded off him before I realized that it was Nova. He grabbed my elbow to steady me but didn't let go. Instead he used it to walk me backward as he advanced forward, moving us back the way I'd come.

"How did you find me?" I blurted, happier to see him than I wanted to let myself be when I knew deep down that he brought bad news.

Nova gazed down at me, anguish flickering in his blood red eyes. "How did you possibly think I couldn't? I told you that you can't run from me."

"I'm not running. I'm right here. Could we slow down a little? Or at least let me see where I'm going." Warm and cozy sensations crept over me, fueled by his touch. He'd proven to both of us that my attraction to him wasn't based on his influence alone. Not anymore. I don't think either of us knew what to do with that.

"I want you, Blaze. I need you." Nova jerked us to a halt then and kissed me hard, a passionate plea. "Now."

I pulled back to meet his gaze, wondering if he'd lost his mind. "Here? Are you serious? Wait, does this mean The Circle wants me dead? Why else would you be willing to take a risk like this?"

"What? No, it's not like that. We can't talk about it here." Nodding toward the throng of people mingling about the lobby, he pulled my hair back to whisper naughtily in my ear, "Let's go upstairs."

Upstairs where the suites were? The look in Nova's eyes told me all I needed to know. He'd come to talk and a lot more than that too. Why else would he find me here, in a place where we could be alone together away from the house?

"Are you sure that's a good idea?" My voice grew breathy as he nuzzled my ear, sucking the lobe into his mouth. Any thoughts of resistance went right out the window.

"I'm not sure about anything anymore, but I'm pretty sure this is a great idea." Between lusty kisses Nova pulled me along to the elevator.

Logic told me to stop him before he could get too deep in my head, among other places. Resisting him got so much harder each time, and I just didn't want to anymore. Especially if The Circle of the Veil was about to have me killed.

The elevator doors had just slid closed, trapping us in together, when I pushed away, struck by a horrible thought. "Are you here to kill me? Is this your way of making it easier?"

To my utter annoyance, Nova burst into boisterous laughter. "Does it look like I'm trying to kill you? Actually I'm trying pretty hard not to fuck you in this elevator."

My face warmed. Pressing my back to the wall of the elevator, I eyed the demon with poorly fueled suspicion. "Why should I believe you?"

Right now Nova was without his demon attributes. Aside from those red eyes, he wore a convincing human guise. It was almost easy to let myself believe he wasn't born of darkness. A demon. Try as I might to let that scare me off, it didn't.

Nova was not a great, all-around upstanding guy. I'd seen examples of that. Hell, I'd been an example of that when he used me as bait. Demons had their own agenda, and they didn't hesitate to act on it. Still, though he was streaked with evil, bits of good emerged. Not all bad, he had tried to help me control my blood magic. He hadn't owed me that in any way, nor did he owe it to me to speak on my behalf in an effort to spare my life.

In a move that stunned me into silence, Nova grabbed my hand and placed it on his hard cock. The fabric of his relaxed other side warrior garb was soft and thin, outlining every amazing inch. "Believe it or not, I don't get hard when I kill, cherry bomb. Trust me, that's not what I'm here to do to you."

With a chime the door slid open. I jerked my hand away but not before the group waiting to enter saw. Damn demon.

Undeterred Nova pulled me along out of the elevator and down the hall to the first empty room we came across. The room was nice, not overtly luxurious but comfortable and clean. Welcoming.

A small couch and coffee table sat across from a flat screen TV on the wall. The window looked out onto the street below. A king-size bed in the corner tempted me to throw caution to the wind and find out why incubus sex was such a big deal.

"Nova, have you lost your mind?" I asked when he locked the door and unfurled his hidden wings. "You said yourself that we can't do this. Isn't the craving already bad enough?"

His tortured crimson gaze drifted over me. "I can't look at you every night and not have you. I've tried. Don't ask me what makes you different than other women or why I have no self-control when it comes to you because I don't fucking know."

My mouth opened but no sound came out. I couldn't process how fast this was happening. Keeping a sober mind in the presence of his intoxicating vibes was especially challenging. I didn't want to keep fighting his pull when Nova was around. His incubus touch might have enhanced the effect, but he'd shielded it completely and I'd still wanted him.

Fuck me. This was happening.

Because I had no words, I let what I felt drive me. Right into his arms, where I wanted to be every time I looked at him. Sliding my arms around Nova's neck, I kissed him, plunging my tongue into his mouth. If we were going to do this, then I didn't see any sense in half-assing it.

My sudden forwardness momentarily surprised him. Tense at first, Nova relaxed into the embrace. As our hungry kiss deepened, he backed me up against the wall between the bed and the couch. Those big wings curled around to trap me on either side. A strong hand captured my jaw as Nova peered into my eyes. His pupils were huge, outlined in the thin red of his iris. His aura buzzed with excitement.

"I'm about to blow your mind and make your pussy scream my name for the rest of your life. But there's just one thing I have to ask first." Nova's hand trailed down to my neck, continuing on down the middle of my body. When he reached my waist, he grabbed each of my wrists in his strong hands, creating an inescapable vice. Gentle but firm, Nova raised my restrained wrists and pressed them to the wall above my head. "Do you trust me?"

A small surge of adrenaline rose up in response to the way he held me bound and trapped. That thrill reminded me that I'd allowed myself to get into what could possibly be a deadly situation without so much as a second thought. Except Nova didn't instill genuine fear within me. Somehow I knew that he'd never hurt me here like this, and my panic never rose.

Not like it had with Rem. Not like it did with true danger.

However, that didn't mean I could trust him with all of me. If I owed Nova anything it was truth. "I trust you with my body, but I still don't trust you with my heart."

The flicker of disappointment in his eyes was eaten up so quickly by lust that I thought I might have imagined it. Releasing my wrists he went for my neck, nipping playfully with fangs that could have torn me to shreds. "Good enough for now."

For now? Had I heard that correctly?

The thought that perhaps allowing this to happen would somehow lead Nova on didn't have the power to stop me. Not when he peeled my clothes off one item at a time and not when he turned me around to face the wall, bent me over, and got on his knees behind me.

Hands on the wall to brace myself, I gasped softly when I felt the heat of his breath against me. Nova gripped my ass, spreading me apart to expose every part of me. "I knew you were a natural redhead," he murmured.

Of course I was, but vampirism had a way of enhancing the colors of hair and eyes. Not that any of that mattered when he followed the observation up with a taste. Just a teasing lick along my wet slit that continued up to include my ass. Surprised at that, I jumped.

Nova's devious chuckle rang all around me. "I am going to have so much fun with you."

My face burned red hot. What the heck had I gotten myself into?

Before I could overthink it, he ran his tongue back the other way to tease my clit. I moaned and twitched away from him, like that would help me to dodge his persistent tongue. Not that I wanted to escape but Nova's touch was intense on a level that bordered on too much. And still, I sensed he was holding back the thrall, keeping its full strength at bay.

Gripping my ass tight to hold me in place, Nova drilled my pussy with his tongue before attacking my clit. Only when I was ready to beg did he ease off my clit to lap at the lusty juices seeping from my entrance. Every pleasure sensation was heightened. Each nerve ending sparked, coming alive in a whole new way. Nova hadn't just been talking with his ego when he claimed that an encounter with him would leave me forever changed.

He brazenly licked my ass again before returning to my clit, sucking it into his mouth. Glancing back, the visual of Nova on his knees, wings tucked in around him as he pleasured me, brought me to a sudden climax. Legs shaking, I whimpered and moaned, needing so much more of him.

His hands left my ass. Once I was able to move, I turned around to find him shirtless, thumbs hooked in his pants as he slid them down. When his cock sprang into view, I licked my lips, a little nervous and a lot ready for every thick inch.

A tattoo on his chest above his heart drew my gaze. About the size of my fist, it was an upside-down star made of twisting vines and thorns. Aside from a long scar that slashed over his ribs on the same side, Nova's body was unmarked. He had a warrior's build: tall and muscular without being bulky or abnormally big. He looked as if someone had made him with painstaking care and detail.

Enamored, I stared at him as if, for the first time in my life, I saw real beauty.

When I failed to do more than lean against the wall and gawk at him, Nova grinned. "Like what you see?"

"You know I do. Why are you holding back? I can tell that you are." Because if Nova had let the thrall run rampant over me the way I knew he could, I wouldn't be able to think so clearly. Did he think I didn't know?

He moved in close so I could feel the heat rolling off his body, pressing his cock against my stomach. A groan escaped him when I wrapped a hand around the shaft. "Because I don't want our first time together to be based on some mindfuck. I want you present here with me. Not to mention that I don't think you can handle everything I can do."

Nice guy and jackass all at once. I could appreciate his honesty though. "That's not for you to decide, but I appreciate your consideration. Really." To show my gratitude I sank to my knees before him and took the head of his cock into my mouth. Peering up at him, I took great satisfaction in the way he cursed softly while tangling a hand in my hair.

"Fuck, I knew your mouth would feel better than any masturbatory fantasy could conjure." Try as he might to withhold his power, the pleasure of my mouth wrapped tight around his shaft made his control slip. The surge of incubus heat that followed caught us both in its powerful grip.

Gathering my hair into a ponytail in one hand, Nova wound it around his fist, holding it up and out of the way so it wouldn't obscure my face. He wanted the full view as I teased the head of his cock with the tip of my tongue before sucking it deep into my mouth. After watching me for as long as he could stand, Nova gently used his grip on my hair to nudge me back to my feet.

I glanced expectantly toward the bed, but Nova just shook his head. Lifting me in his arms, he put my back against the wall, holding tight to my ass. His cock strained between us, rubbing against my entrance but not yet slipping inside.

Our eyes met and my breath stopped.

Nova saw me suck in a breath and hold it. A dark brow quirked in question. "Still all on board, cherry bomb? I can stop, but I'd much rather nail you to the wall."

"That's pretty fucking romantic," I deadpanned, batting my eyes sarcastically before rolling them. "I don't want you to stop. I want you to quit holding back and blow my fucking mind already. Isn't that kind of your thing, dark star?"

Nova's pupils widened like a cat right before it pounces. He thrust into me, easing his way in rather than forcing it, something I was grateful for when I felt how large he was inside me. My body gave him a slick, warm passage.

"Is this what you want?" he growled softly, letting his hold on the thrall slip further.

My ears rang like I'd just walked out of a rock concert as the room filled with sex-charged power. It was everywhere, climbing inside me, making me think, feel, and want nothing but Nova. All of him in all of me. As deep as he could get.

Holding onto him like it was the only thing keeping me grounded, I moaned, "Yes. Oh my God, yes. Don't stop."

If he noticed my little faux pas, he didn't let on. Maybe he even liked it. Holding my ass tight enough to leave bruises, Nova fucked me up against the wall until my moans became cries. Every cell was filled with him, like the way we touched was more than physical. More than sex.

When Nova pulled out and placed me back on my feet, I thought surely now we'd head for the bed. But no, the filthy incubus bent me over the arm of the couch and entered me from behind. The sound of feathers rustling about had become familiar. A cool breeze caressed my upraised rear end as his wings flapped gently a few times before resettling.

The static in my ears grew to a steady roar of white noise. Through it I could hear Nova's heavy breaths and moans. Every stroke of his body into mine seemed to increase the power in the room until I saw through a haze of lust and heard myself begging for more. It was pretty safe to say that he'd stopped holding back.

Nova pumped several more times before withdrawing again, something that was starting to become a real tease. The touch of his tongue gliding over my ass and down my slit sent a quiver through me. I gave a little squeal of surprise when he followed up with a firm smack on my behind before sweeping me off my feet and carrying me to the bed.

"Don't think I didn't see you eyeing the bed, you lazy vixen." Nova laid me down gently, but as he hovered over me on the bed, his hand slid around my throat, pinning me down beneath him.

I blinked dopey eyes, a silly smile crossing my face. Nova's thrall was a drug like no other. "Just didn't expect you to want to do me on every inch of this hotel room before we made it to the bed. I mean look at this thing. It was made for sex."

As Nova stared down at me his face took on a tender, somewhat wistful expression. His power was a strange thing, as it seemed to consume him as much as it consumed me. Lost so fully inside the magic that held us, Nova crushed his lips to mine and roughly thrust inside me.

Above us his wings stretched out to create a black canopy like the darkest, starless night. I drank in the sight of Nova, all of him. From the horns curving off the top of his head to the tail that whipped about behind him, I enjoyed every part.

The molten lava spilling through his eyes made me his willing captive. An otherworldly passion consumed me. I opened myself fully to Nova, letting him possess my body with total abandon. So deep under his influence was I that he could've done pretty much anything to me at that point and I'd have let him.

But the passion consumed Nova too. He gathered me close, pressing his face into my neck, breathing sexy groans in my ear. Faster he moved, filling me harder and deeper, until his name was a cry on my lips.

Everything within him fed upon this moment. The intimacy. The lust. The power of orgasmic release. I felt him pull from me as he gave back, creating a cycle of pleasure that brought us both to greater heights.

I came with an explosion of rapture that threw my head back and turned my cries to screams. Nova didn't let himself come yet. Pushing himself up over me so he could look down at my face, the tender passion he'd shown vanished. With a hand on my shoulder and another in my splayed hair, Nova held me down beneath him and fucked me with savage wildness. Only when he had me twitching around his cock with orgasm yet again did he fill me with his release.

Nova rolled onto his back next to me on the bed, tucking his wings beneath him. He left several inches between us but reached over to take my hand. Maybe it was the strange high playing with my head, but he seemed unsure of how to proceed from here, now that we'd crossed the forbidden line. Or maybe he was the fuck-and-leave type, and now this would get awkward.

For several long minutes we didn't speak. He just slid his fingers through mine and held my hand tight. The room felt off center, like we'd knocked the entire planet askew. Gradually the sensation of floating receded and the haze cleared.

"I have bad news." Nova broke the after-sex silence in the worst way in the history of ever.

"Don't tell me. You're married. They always wait until the sex is over to confess." My attempt at humor brought a tight, pinched smile to his face.

This was the part where he told me what The Circle decided to do with me. Great timing. So much for the afterglow.

Nova tore his gaze from the ceiling to meet mine. "The only way I could keep them off your back was to tell them about your blood magic. They've decided to hand down a punishment for keeping it from them, but you're the one who has to face the challenge."

"What?" I shot upright, my relaxed calm gone like it had never been. "How the hell is that a punishment for you?"

"They suspect I've formed some kind of attachment to you. Why else would I hide something from them? This is how they punish us both." Using our joined hands, Nova tugged me back down and pulled me in against him.

"So what's the punishment?" I muttered against his chest, eyeing the ink over his heart. Try as I might, I couldn't relax completely. "It must be bad since you waited until now to tell me."

Nova wrapped his arms and a wing around me, folding me in a blanket of feathers. "They want you to go back into the FPA base and get some kind of proof that we either do or don't have a spy in our house. Alone."

Despite the heat of Nova's body at my side, a chill ran through me. "How am I supposed to do that? They're setting me up to fail."

His tail coiled around my ankle, fuzzy and soft on my skin. "You can do it. We'll make it work. Most of their manpower leaves every night. I can orchestrate a distraction to ensure they all leave. You'll only have the security staff to deal with."

I propped myself on an elbow so I could search his eyes, though for what I wasn't yet sure. "It can't possibly be that easy."

"Oh, it won't be easy, but if anyone can do it, it's you. You're the strongest one in the house right now, Blaze. Once The Circle sees how valuable you are, they'll back off. So you have to show them." Nova pulled me in for a tender kiss that was affectionate rather than straight up lusty.

Naming me as the strongest on the team might have been a stretch. At least Ghost could control his magic. "I can see why you waited until after to tell me. Bad news is kind of a mood killer."

"I don't know about that. I'm ready for round two. We're not leaving this room until you come at least three more times." Waggling dark brows, Nova chuckled, his red eyes especially bright. "But I suppose I should tell you my theory first."

"Theory?" I repeated, afraid to hear it.

"About your blood magic and your aura, why it's so dark and demonic in nature." Touching my face, Nova grew serious. "I haven't spoken a word of this to anyone, cherry bomb, but I think before you became a vampire, you were a nephilim."

The beat of his heart was loud in my ears, though not as loud as that word echoing over and over. Nephilim. Half human and half immortal, fathered by either an angel or a demon, a human with the powers of an immortal on a lesser scale.

"But how could that be?" I struggled to make sense of his theory. "My father was—"

"A man who sold you off the first chance he got because you were never really his to begin with and he knew it." Nova paused, caressing my cheek as it all sunk in. "Most immortals who father an illegitimate child with a human are imprisoned. It's a crime. This is still a theory, Blaze, but it's one I'll chase down if you want. It would explain your blood magic and why it's so wild."

Not to mention my red aura, a color only demons have apparently. Fathered by an immortal? How could such a thing even be possible? Would my mother not have told me? She and my father had slept in separate bedrooms since I was a child. Could that have been why?

Nova had just thrown a lot at me. Too much to let fully sink in while laying on a bed naked next to him. Climbing on top of him, I raked my hands down his hard chest. "Let's come back to that later. I'm more interested in those three orgasms."

I had to be. If I let myself go too far down the rabbit hole with Nova's theory, I might discover something I'd never be ready to learn.

CHAPTER TWENTY-TWO

RAYNE

T he three of you will bait the FPA and lead them on a chase. Keep them busy." Nova pointed to Tavi, Ghost, and Corr. "I'll be across town setting another trap for them. The goal is to keep every one of their teams busy. We want that building as empty for Blaze as we can get it."

The six of us stood around the large kitchen island. Next to me Blaze leaned on the counter, playing it cool despite the nerves she'd confessed to me when we'd been alone. She'd come in the previous morning just before sunrise looking guilty as hell and stinking of Nova. Now the two of them could barely make eye contact across the island.

So that had happened. I didn't love it, but I did love that she never had that guilty look on her face after leaving my room.

After hearing from Blaze all about The Circle of the Veil's punishment task, I'd been pissed. This was all Nova's fault. He'd been making personal decisions regarding her right from the start. Maybe I couldn't blame him for seeing in her what I saw, but he was the superior here. If he couldn't stick to that task, then perhaps he shouldn't be here anymore.

"And you," he continued, pointing at me. "You'll drop her off near the base and remain in the vicinity. If she doesn't come out by dawn, go in after her."

"Let me guess," I added, keeping my inner wolf on a leash. "If she dies, I die. That's the rule now, isn't it?"

Maybe I shouldn't have said it, but I was pissed off. Fed up with Nova's ego, I had to call him out before he sent Blaze into a deadly situation.

Blaze peered back and forth across the island between us. "Um, excuse me? What does that mean?" When neither of us volunteered more, she added, "Nobody here is responsible for anything that happens to me, Nova."

Except maybe the demon himself. He seemed to be responsible for The Circle's punishment. I let myself enjoy it when she hit Nova with an especially harsh warning glare.

Pretending like he didn't want to leap across the island and strangle me to death, Nova continued. "Give us an hour to clear the building. Then go in. Upstairs is the control room. There will be some security in the building, but most of it will be in the basement. Go up, copy any hard drives you can gain access to. Threaten, abuse, I don't care. Do whatever it takes if you need passwords or keycards."

Nova rambled on a little longer, covering bases with the others and answering the questions Tavi threw at him. She'd been in a real mood since the full moon two nights ago. She hadn't wanted to come with Corr and me. She only shifted when she couldn't fight it anymore. Then she'd ran like hell through the forest and hadn't returned until morning, her muzzle bloody from a kill.

Like everyone else here, Tavi had some issues to work on. If she could learn to make her human and wolf sides work together, she'd be even more of a badass. Still she wasn't afraid of the challenges we faced here nightly. Already her eyes shone with eagerness for tonight's mission.

I wished I could feel the same. All I felt was a barely repressed rage that tonight had to happen at all. Blaze deserved better.

After the others left I was alone with Nova and Blaze. He held us back in the foyer.

"Do whatever it takes to get what you need and get out of there." He pressed a thumb drive into Blaze's hand. "And for fuck's sakes, cherry bomb, use the damn symbols I showed you."

He pulled her in close, and I took that as my cue to head out to the garage. Nova's closeness to Blaze didn't threaten me. It worried me. Demons couldn't be trusted. An incubus demon could be trusted even less.

I pulled the black Charger out of the garage and into the driveway. I hadn't expected to see the car again after it was left in the street during Ghost and Blaze's arrest. She joined me a few minutes later, her face pulled into a tight frown.

"Drive slow." She let her head drop back against the seat. "Take the long way. I am not in a rush to get there."

"You got it." Anything to keep from delivering her right to an enemy. The Circle of the Veil had said that Nova couldn't help her. They hadn't explicitly said anything about me.

Blaze's dainty but deadly strong hand crept across the console between us to slide onto my thigh. A silent plea for reassurance graced her touch. Keeping one hand on the steering wheel, I covered hers with the other. When she remained quiet for several blocks, I said, "If you want to talk, I'm all ears."

"Just can't help but feel like this is some kind of trick, you know? Like The Circle is sending me in there so that I become the FPA's problem, not theirs." She laughed bitterly. "They expect me to fail."

"Nobody else does though," I offered, trying to flip the way she viewed her circumstances. Not that I'd have felt any different in her shoes. "I believe you'll get in and out, no problem. Nova must believe it too, or he'd be more of a dick than usual."

"Yeah right," she scoffed. "Why would he expect you to swoop in and save my ass then? What a jerkwad move."

As wary as I was of Nova's interest in Blaze, I couldn't bring myself to be a dick about it. "He can't be everywhere at once. I guess it's his way of keeping you safe. Or trying to. Clearly, the asshole cares about you. Between you and me, I don't think he's familiar with the feeling."

She chuckled then, a laugh filled with genuine mirth. Turning to me in the dark of the car she asked, "What's going on with you two anyway? I thought I'd have to break you guys up with the way you were glaring at each other. Is it because of me? 'Cause I don't want that, Rayne."

"No worries, babe. We disliked each other before you showed up. It's nothing personal. He's just a hard guy to get along with, especially when he's pulling rank." I gave her hand a warm squeeze, rubbing the back of her fingers. Then I brought her hand up and sucked the tip of her pinky finger into my mouth.

It got her laughing again and squirming in her seat. As we drove through the city I took as many side roads and alternate paths I could. Once Nova and the others had drawn the FPA out, we'd get an alert from the watchdog team, but nearing our destination made my fingers tighten on the wheel.

"I was in love once," I heard myself say, cringing as the past drove me to address the present. "Her name was Sadie. After the attack, I couldn't face her with the truth, and I couldn't lie to her forever. So I left."

Blaze listened attentively, leaning in her seat to better see me as I told the story about how I'd left Sadie behind. To protect her. I wasn't sure why this felt like the right time to tell Blaze about it. Maybe because I'd spent a long time thinking about all the things I never got to say.

When I finished I ended with, "I'm falling for you, Blaze. And it scares the shit out of me. I don't want to fuck things up this time."

"Pull over."

Her command surprised me. We'd just turned into the residential neighborhood that housed the FPA base. I pulled the car to a stop and put it in park.

Blaze grabbed my face with both hands and forced me to look into her tranquil blue eyes. How she managed to be so calm right now I didn't know. With a coy smile she said, "I'm in like with you too."

Then her mouth was on mine, saying more than either of us were ready to voice aloud. But I couldn't just let her walk in there without saying anything at all. Letting her into my past felt vulnerable but right. Her reference to our silly inside joke chased away any ill will I'd felt toward Nova's attraction to her. Whatever they had, they could have it. It would never replicate what I shared with her. This was unique only to us.

When she pulled back a new expression had stolen over her features, one I'd come to know as her game face. "You're the first person to make me feel safe in as long as I can remember. Like I can let down my guard with you. I'm scared too, Rayne, but I'm still in this for one night at a time if you are."

We'd agreed to take things by the day, since we couldn't see further ahead than that anyway. Hearing her voice so much trust in me hit home, and it hit hard. Hard enough that I had to stuff down the emotion it evoked. Now wasn't the time. She had to go. Any minute now.

"You know I am, beauty." I kissed her again, ignoring the awkwardness of the console between us.

My phone went off with the alert I'd been dreading.

Blaze wore a matching disappointed frown. "I'll just get out here. Don't let anyone see you."

I pulled her in for one more kiss before responding to the message, confirming it had been received. "Hey, I know that Nova said sunrise, but I'm not waiting that long. If I don't hear from you in an hour, I'm coming in. The Circle never said specifically that I couldn't help you, only that Nova couldn't. Not that I think you need help. But you shouldn't have to do this at all, let alone by yourself."

Blaze paused while double checking that she had everything she'd need inside. "You don't have to do that. Really. It's cool."

"I do though. Even if you could convince me to stay put, you couldn't convince the wolf." I flashed her a cheeky grin before shoving her playfully toward the door. Though all I wanted to do was lock the doors and hit the road, just get out of here. Away. Fuck The Circle of the Veil. Fuck all of them.

She'd never do it though, run off and leave the others behind at Mayhem House, which was why I would never ask. Werewolves might be many things, but when we knew who our family was, our loyalty stood the test of time. I'd follow Blaze to the ends of the earth and back if she asked.

"Let me know when you get into the control room if you can," I said as she got out of the car. "I'll stay close enough to grab you as soon as you get out. If I don't hear from you, well, you know."

"Stay out of trouble, you big bad wolf." With a wink, she closed the door and disappeared into the night. Vampires had an uncanny way of doing that, just becoming the night.

Keeping on the move was safer than staying in the same place this close to FPA turf. Reluctantly, I put the car in gear and glided down the street. I couldn't stop glancing at the time on the dash.

That hour started now.

CHAPTER TWENTY-THREE

Leaving Rayne after the talk we'd had felt wrong. If anything it made me that much more determined to pull this off and get back to him in one piece. Within an hour.

Rayne had said he'd come in after me, and as much as I appreciated the wolf's deep loyalty, I couldn't let him risk himself for me. Although, if it took more than an hour to do this, my odds of getting out unscathed were incredibly slim.

Moving among the shadows I drew closer to the looming hospital. Fuck, it looked like a horror movie waiting to happen. Glancing around at the many houses nearby, I couldn't help but wonder who wanted to see that thing out their window every night. The street was deathly quiet. Like nobody ventured out after dark in this part of the city. Following the darkness and avoiding the streetlights, I stepped onto the grounds, hating the sudden sinking sensation that followed.

Too many spirits here.

Being back so soon felt a little daunting. But nobody knew I was here yet, and the longer I could keep it that way, the better my chances of doing this. My biggest concern was the thumb drive in my jeans pocket. What if I couldn't find the proof they needed? What then?

I slipped up on the closest side of the building and made my way around to the same door Ghost and I had been taken in through. The stairs there led to the top floor where Nova said the control room would be.

Before entering the building, I paused to ensure I was still alone. Then I pulled out the new phone Nova gave me to replace the one I'd lost and set a timer for forty-five minutes. Just to keep me on task.

Stuffing the phone in my back pocket, I pulled the bullet-deflecting dagger Nova had given me from its sheath and put my other hand on the door handle. Would an alarm go off when I opened it? Would I be fucked before I could even get started?

Nova wasn't allowed to help me, so even though I could take the dagger along, he couldn't give me any charms, amulets, or other handy trinkets. Not this time. He'd encouraged me to use the symbols he'd shown me. To be honest, I only remembered the illusion symbol. Still, if I could muster more than savage bunnies, maybe it would prove useful. Or make me look like a total idiot. One or the other.

Gritting my teeth, I opened the door. It wasn't even locked. No alarm. Unless it was a silent alarm. I didn't wait around to find out. Opening the door just wide enough for me to slip inside, I headed right for the stairwell I'd glimpsed during my last visit. Time was ticking.

The stairwell proved a danger zone and an obstacle course all in one. And so damn dark. Unnaturally so. It took my eyes a moment to adjust, and even then I had a hard time picking my way through the rubble that littered the stairs. A psi ball glowing in my palm helped me see that it was mostly construction debris that snagged at my feet. Broken window shards gleamed in the red light of my energy ball.

My demon energy ball. Because apparently I was fathered by a demon. A fucking demon.

Nova could have been lying, and he had said it was just a theory. Still it would explain so much.

Sharp objects were not my friends. I knew that I'd probably have to bleed to get out of here, but I wanted it to be on my terms. Which was why I'd used a permanent marker to draw the illusion symbol on the palm of my left hand.

By the time I reached the top of what had to be seven or eight flights of stairs, it felt like it had taken hours. According to my phone it had been eight minutes. Still too long.

I paused at the door at the top. One of the doors was supposed to be alarmed, but I didn't know which. "Here goes nothing."

The door was locked, but after a little telekinetic push it opened without incident. Entering a hallway much cleaner than the death stairs, I made my way toward the light at one end. Several sets of heavy security doors separated me from the control room. One of them, at least, would be alarmed. I needed a plan that didn't include busting my way in. Every agent in the building would be on me then.

If they hadn't already picked up sight of me on their cameras, they soon would. I could try to pass myself off as one of them, but that seemed risky. Keeping my back pressed to the wall, I moved down the dark hallway. The only light coming in streamed through the windows. The electricity didn't run throughout the entire building.

For this to work I needed an agent to open the security doors. I didn't want to wait—no time for that—but wait I did. Back pressed to the wall, I watched the light at the end of the hall. Eventually someone had to come in or out, right?

Two ghostly soldiers emerged from the wall beside me, making me jump. I clapped a hand over my mouth to muffle a startled shriek. They didn't acknowledge me. In unison they marched down the hallway before disappearing into mist. So much unrest in this place. I could feel the presence of the bigger, darker force deep down below. Sitting back, it watched me.

I was about to text Rayne to extend his hour when a man in a suit with a gun on his hip came striding down the hall toward me from the control room. Using a swipe card he made it through the alarmed security doors with no problem.

As he drew closer to where I stood cloaked in shadow, he paused to radio to someone to grab another agent and check the basement. "There's nobody up here."

Crap. They knew I was here. Of course they did. They were the Feds. Waiting for him to get closer was killing me, especially when he kept stopping and glancing back the way he'd come. Just a little closer.

One more step and then he saw me. Eyes wide, he fumbled for both his gun and his radio. Out of the darkness I lunged at him. Moving too fast for his human eyes to follow, I slid around behind him and slashed the dagger blade across his throat.

Sure I could have taken him as a hostage instead, but that would only send the message that I was willing to negotiate. And I wasn't. Not tonight. This was dog eat dog. Knocking him out would only let him creep up behind me later. I wasn't taking any chances.

Swiping the guy's keycard, I left him to bleed out on the floor and made my way quickly through the security doors. I knew that if the Feds inside the building had figured out I was on the top floor, they'd be on their way. I had to hurry.

I burst into the control room to find a bank of monitors and computers manned by four people. They'd seen me coming on the screens. Two of them held guns, another grabbed for the phone.

Slapping the phone out of her hand, I jerked her close and pressed the bloody dagger blade to her neck. So much for not taking a hostage. Fishing the thumb drive from my pocket, I tossed it to the closest guy.

"Everything you have on the agents you employ, put it on that thing. Don't leave anything out. You have thirty seconds or I slit her throat." With my life on the line, I held nothing back. I couldn't afford to.

I half expected them to put up a fight or take a shot anyway, but they responded calmly, likely having trained for such an incident. The man closest to me slowly leaned forward and bent down to retrieve the drive. Another man nodded, and the first stuck it into his computer.

"Is that all you want?" asked a curly-haired guy with glasses. "Because we'll give it to you. Nobody has to get hurt. Please."

His gentle plea made me feel bad about the guy back in the hall. But one even-toned Fed didn't suddenly make them the good guys. They'd take the first chance they could to kill me.

"Twenty-five seconds." I tightened my grip on the woman.

She didn't make a move or say a word. Hands held up beside her, she seemed to be doing all she could not to trigger my predatory instincts. Smart.

"It's coming; it's coming." The man copying the files waved a hand at the screen like that would make it go faster.

Maybe it did. A few seconds later he ejected the drive and tossed it back to me. "Pick it up and hand it to me," I instructed the woman. "Slowly. Don't try anything else."

Once the drive was back in my pocket, I eased toward the door, dragging the woman with me. In the doorway I let her go and ran back down the hall, slamming through the security doors with the key card held ready. If the agents in the control room didn't come after me, those from the basement surely would.

Skittering down the decrepit stairs back to the ground floor, I couldn't move as carefully as I had on the way up. I skipped several stairs at a time, picking my way through the cluttered landings to the next flight. When I reached the bottom, I paused to find a small shard of glass, knowing I'd need it, whether I wanted to or not.

Glass in one hand, dagger in the other, I crept around the corner into the tiny entryway I'd come through. Something had me on high alert. I rounded the corner expecting to find a fleet of crossbow pistols pointed at me. The entryway was empty. Still instinct had served me long enough to know when someone was sneaking up on me.

There was only one way out from here, and that was the door I'd come through. Aside from the stairwell, there was an elevator, but I sure as hell wasn't taking it down below.

Staring at the door that led outside, back to certain freedom, I knew without a doubt there were Feds on the other side, waiting for me to come out. If Nova and the others had succeeded in luring most of their people to various locations around the city, then hopefully there wouldn't be many.

No putting this off.

Ducking back into the base of the stairwell, I sucked in a breath of harsh, musty air. I stared at the glass shard, willing myself to do this with ease, take command of what was mine. Stop being afraid. Fear whispered in my ear, telling me that I was trapped, that there was no way out.

"Fuck this shit," I muttered, anger rising in response to that fear. "And fuck The Circle of the Veil for putting me in this position."

Beneath me the dark spirit slithered closer. Its genderless voice oozed power in my ear as it murmured one word: "Bleed."

Even it knew what I had to do to get out of here alive. And alive it would be, even if I had to take out every person that stood in my way. I was a survivor. And whether my birth father was a demon or I was just unlucky, it didn't matter. The blood magic had saved my life many times. Though it might have hurt many people, it had never hurt me. It protected me. I couldn't fear its explosive nature anymore. I had to harness it.

Steeling myself, I sliced a small gash in my forearm and dropped the shard. I'd wait until I'd made it outside to use the illusion symbol. Using the charge of the blood that spilled from the cut, I sheathed the dagger and headed for the door with both hands raised for a telekinetic hit.

Without letting myself hesitate or think at all, I just acted. Kicking the door open, I released a supercharged shock of energy that slammed into the waiting agents. Thanks to my team's efforts, there were only four of them.

My attack took three of them down. I pulled my dagger free in time to block the shot the fourth agent took at me, hitting him with a counter shot of my own. In my peripheral view I saw a black SUV pull up. Two more agents burst out the door I'd just exited, and I turned to hit them with a large psi ball.

As I nailed some, others recovered. Rayne would be coming soon, and I couldn't have him happen upon this scene. The blood had only been enough for one shot. This would require more than a few drops.

"Stop resisting or we will shoot to kill." One of the Feds shouted at me, but they were all in dark suits, weapons aimed.

I didn't know who ordered me to surrender, and I didn't care. It wasn't happening.

The occupants of the newly arrived SUV had yet to get out. I'd have found it odd if I didn't have six crossbow pistols aimed at my heart and head. First things first.

I held the dagger ready, its blade glowing protective gold. I needed an opportunity to flee without giving them a chance to give chase. Driven by nothing but the need to survive if only to finally get the chance to laugh in The Circle's face because they were so wrong about me, I dragged the glowing blade over my wrist.

The gash that opened up was much bigger than the small slice I'd made with the glass. The blood magic bubbled up like lava, and I hurriedly smeared blood on the illusion symbol in my palm while envisioning a pack of vicious dogs. I wasn't crazy enough to try for a dragon or something fantastical like that.

Six growling, red-eyed rottweilers suddenly surrounded me. Lips peeled back into angry snarls, they exploded forward, driven by the force of my magic, lunging at the Feds. Screams rang out as agents were wrestled to the ground by imaginary dogs that felt and acted real. Those still on their feet either ran for the door or turned their weapons on the dogs, a futile effort.

I couldn't be sure how long my magic would keep the dogs going, but already I felt the draw. The blood magic always left me drained.

The timer on my phone went off, a small chime and vibration from my back pocket to let me know that I had to get gone now. Before Rayne or anybody else could come along.

Surrounding myself in an energy circle, I channeled the rest of my magic into making it a sturdy barrier to protect me as I ran for it. I turned to go and caught sight of a woman leaning against the front of the SUV. A dark-haired werewolf, this had to be Agent Juliet O'Brien. I'd wondered when our paths would cross.

She never moved. Arms crossed, she watched me retreat, leaving her crew to flee a pack of magical demon dogs. Across the distance, twenty feet or more, our eyes met. Her expression revealed nothing. No reaction to the attack on her colleagues and no attempt to come after me. What was up with that?

I didn't stick around to find out. I bolted down the street and over several blocks before I paused in someone's backyard long enough to call Rayne. While I waited for him to pick me up, I turned the thumb drive over and over in my bloodstained hands.

If The Circle of the Veil didn't find what they wanted on this drive, would they still kill me? Would they do it just to punish Nova? I couldn't help but feel that proving to them I could get in and out of that building was a mistake I would pay for later.

CHAPTER TWENTY-FOUR

Stretching out in my bed felt amazing after the last few nights of mayhem. Spending a solid twenty-four hours in my room was a treat to myself. A little self-care. Luckily, I didn't spend them alone. Dalyn sat on one side of me, propped against the headboard, blankets drawn up. On my other side Corr relaxed with one arm beneath his head. Rayne sprawled across the foot of the bed on his stomach, clutching a pillow, a small bite visible on his neck from last night when he'd so generously donated to help me bounce back. We were a few hours into a *Lord of the Rings* movie marathon.

My bedroom smelled of werewolves, satsuma perfume, and popcorn. Mostly popcorn. That shit had a way of overtaking every other aroma.

Since making it back to the house relatively unscathed last night, I'd cycled through a mix of emotions: Satisfied that I'd done what The Circle hadn't expected me to pull off. Terrified that they'd hate me for it. Not to mention the worry that they knew Nova and I were involved. They would use it against us.

My current mood was content, but being snuggled in with the people I cared most about made me worry for them too. Tavi had slipped out alone tonight. She'd been her usual surly self, telling Dalyn and me to mind our damn business when we asked where she was going. It led to a few snarky jokes from Ghost after she'd left about her being the spy. But he'd left on his own personal outing too, so who was he to talk?

Nova had promised us a few nights of down time while the watchdog crew reviewed the thumb drive. We all needed it. I'd hoped to see him tonight, but since retrieving the thumb drive from me last night, he hadn't been around. There were so many things I needed to discuss with him.

"Fuck this ring." Rayne threw popcorn at the TV mounted on the wall, which only succeeded in scattering popcorn on the floor. "They need to lock that thing in a box and bury it in the middle of nowhere. Salt the earth and forget about it."

"You can't do that, numb nuts," Dalyn scoffed, biting the head off a gummy worm. "It's a magic ring. It would find a way out. Trust me, you can't fuck with magic rings."

"Sounds like you have a good story." Corr's lazy observation invited her to share, but she shook her head.

Waving a hand, Dalyn laughed, but it was secretive as hell. "A story I promised to take to the grave. Don't even ask."

This girl just kept getting better and better. I didn't think there was a person in this house who wasn't a complex tangle of quirks and darkness. A mysterious bunch, I adored them far more than I'd ever intended.

"Don't even ask?" Rayne echoed, pushing himself into a half sitting position. "You can't make claims about magic rings without backing it up. Start talking, Christina."

Rayne's joking reference to her young, Christina Aguilera-ish appearance did it for Dalyn. She paused the movie before throwing the remote at him. He laughed when it fell short, landing on the bed.

"And on that note, I need some real food," she said, climbing out of the bed. "I'm going down to the kitchen to make some mac n' cheese."

"Take your garbage with you." I gathered her popcorn bag and chocolate bar wrapper, shoving it at her.

Dalyn clambered over me and Corr before hopping down to the floor. Accepting the trash with a grimace, she shuffled out of the room. Left alone with the two werewolves, I was more than ready to get cuddly with both of them. Well, Corr and I shared an attraction, but it hadn't yet reached that point. So when all he did was hold my hand, that was enough for me.

"I'm gonna hit the pool for a swim." Rayne rolled off the bed, waggling both brows at me. "It doesn't look like I can convince you to join me, so let me know when you guys start the movie back up."

"I'll be sure to shout out the window at you," I joked with a wink, settling into the blankets a little deeper at the thought of the cold pool water.

Rayne paused in the doorway. "And I'll be sure you get a hell of a view when you do." Then he was gone, the sound of his feet thumping down the stairs followed.

"Do you need a break too?" I rolled onto my side to better face Corr. "You could probably get in on Dalyn's mac n' cheese. Or squeeze in a few chapters on whatever book you're reading now."

"Actually, I was hoping to get some time alone with you." Corr followed my lead and burrowed deeper under the blankets. "I didn't get a chance to answer your question. Back in the cemetery. About why I'm here."

Other than our joined hands we didn't touch, but he was close enough for me to feel the heat rolling off him. Selfishly, I wanted to know why everyone was in this house. Who wouldn't? I didn't want him to feel any obligation to open up, but I sensed that maybe he needed to unburden himself.

"I'm all ears, handsome." I gave his hand an encouraging squeeze.

Corr readjusted his pillow so we were face to face, a few inches between us. At this distance his dark lashes, enviously long and full, beautifully framed his gray-blue eyes. I could so easily fall into them.

"The wolf who turned me was from the gym I trained at. He was part of an underground fight ring. Werewolves against humans who had no idea they were fighting wolves. Of course they could never beat us. Rich assholes came to bet on the fights, having no idea what was going on. The guys running the thing took a cut and made a fuck ton. They made sure every wolf got their fair share too, so long as we kept showing up to fight." He paused, uncertainty skipping over his face before he added, "I kept showing up. Even when shit got crazy and people started dying. Death fights make a killing, you know."

His voice broke. He swallowed hard but didn't look away, like he needed to see whatever might show in my eyes, my initial reaction to his admission. If he expected judgment, then he didn't realize how many deaths an almost century old vampire had on their hands.

"So you were a willing turn," I prodded, gently urging him to continue. When we'd first met I'd assumed that he'd been attacked. He hadn't corrected me. "How did The Circle find you?"

"Someone on the inside leaked it to the FPA, of all things." Corr laughed as a memory stole over his face. "The Circle found out through the watchdog team's close eye on the Feds. The night the Feds came to raid the place, The Circle sent Nova and a few others to chase them off. Most of the wolves ran or were hunted by the elites. Those who stayed were given a choice."

"Same choice I was given. Come here or die." I nodded knowingly. "How many of you were there?"

"Nine. It wasn't a large organization, but it drew a large enough crowd. I'm the only one who came willingly." Corr's tone hollowed with a sadness he hadn't let himself feel yet. He pushed it aside again as a small half smile curved his lips. "I didn't want to be here, but I wasn't ready to die. I'm glad I came though. It broke me out of a life I shouldn't have been living. Too many years on the streets after my parents died, too many bad decisions. It's a miracle I'm still alive."

No way could I imagine everything Corr had lived through, just like he could never really know what I'd faced. All we could do was listen to each other, and that seemed to be enough.

"For what it's worth, I'm glad you came too." When a lock of hair flopped onto his forehead, I reached to brush it away without thinking.

His pupils dilated, and the steady thud of his pulse picked up tempo. "You're really easy to talk to, Blaze, and as much as I'm dying to kiss you right now, I don't want to step on another wolf's toes. So to speak." The wolf peered out of Corr, reminding me that I cozied up next to a wild beast. "Not that I think you belong to him or any misogynistic shit like that, but it's no secret how much time you spend together."

It baffled me how a guy as intelligent and respectful as Corr had waged underground death fights. Though most people would never believe half the shit I'd done either. Do monsters ever really look like monsters? No, that would make life far too easy.

"We've grown close," I confirmed, touching his socked foot with mine. "But let's just say that Rayne's pretty good at sharing. None of us are in the position for dating and finding our happy ever after. Not in this place. So why not enjoy whatever we find within these walls?"

Corr's eyes took on a gray hue that was almost silver as the edges of his iris seeped slowly into wolf. The beat of his heart thudded faster. "I'm not good at this stuff. I've never been in anything serious, and I definitely have not been in a situation like this."

"Just follow your instinct and do what feels right. We're not getting out of here alive, so we might as well live in the mo—"

He cut me off with a kiss, careful at first, like he didn't want to rush it. Corr didn't open up quickly. I'd discovered that myself. I expected it to be the same with physical affection, and that was fine with me. Good things were worth waiting for.

The cool, sporty cologne he wore mixed with the scent of wolf to create an aroma that was just Corr. It teamed up with his heartbeat to make me wonder what he tasted like. I could hear the blood rushing through his veins, begging to be set free. There may have been a possibility that I'd taken too much blood from Rayne recently. It was starting to get to my head.

Corr's kiss grew more intense. His tongue slipped between my lips, and I welcomed it. When he touched the side of my face before slipping a hand into my loose tendrils, I melted against him.

The quiet wolf claimed my mouth with a calm but commanding kiss that ended with me momentarily disoriented. I stared at him like a moron while trying to make words happen.

Corr beat me to it, snuggling in closer. "I get to ask the next question."

CHAPTER TWENTY-FIVE

S o it turns out that the thumb drive Blaze stole is completely useless." Standing at the heading of the dining room table, Nova waited for that to sink in. "It doesn't tell us anything we didn't already know. Agent names, addresses, former locations. Useless shit."

My stomach twisted itself into a pretzel of knots. All that had been for nothing. The Circle of the Veil had no reason to keep me around. Not if they already thought I was a liability. And if they didn't think so due to my blood magic, they surely would because of Nova's obvious attachment to me.

"However," Nova continued, his crimson gaze slashing over me and away, "I'm not one to accept defeat so easily. I did get the information I wanted, although I'm not about to share exactly how, and I do know which one of you is our spy."

I hadn't wanted to believe there was a spy in the house, but there was no other way to account for the Feds knowing how to find us so easily on recent outings. Everyone waited for Nova to make the big reveal.

Next to me Ghost stretched and leaned back in his chair, not in the least worried. Not that I'd ever have pegged him for a spy. Heartbeats were loud in the silence, especially the human hearts. Dalyn sat stiff, staring at Nova. But it was Ira's erratic heart rate that tipped me off before Nova outed him.

"Ira, would you care to tell us why you went to the FPA and volunteered to be an informant? I'm especially interested in how you thought you'd get away with it." The hooded sleeveless tunic Nova wore showed off his sculpted arms. He crossed them, wings flared out behind him, and ambled slowly around the table toward the older witch.

"I don't know what you're talking about." Ira stayed calm on the outside, but his thumping heartbeat sounded worrisome.

Nova's chuckle was so sinister, it made the tiny hairs on the back of my neck stand on end, and he wasn't even looking at me. "I'm going to kill you either way. This is your only chance to explain why you sold out your team."

The air seemed to get sucked out of the room. Tavi, who sat next to Ira, got up and rounded the table to stand on the opposite side. Couldn't blame her, I'd have cleared out too.

Ira watched the demon draw closer, and his pulse pounded harder. It echoed in my head. The stink of fear that surrounded him made him nothing but prey to my bloodlust. Not a great time to be reminded that I needed a good kill.

"After I got shot," Ira shouted, voice raised in panic. "I have a family. They have nothing without me. The Circle doesn't care about them, but the Feds promised them protection and enough money to get by. If any of you were in my position, you'd have done the same."

Not one of us could argue, but we weren't in Ira's place. Wouldn't we all do what we felt we had to for those we loved? I had never had that life. A family. Not really.

Nova's voice dripped venom when he said, "I sincerely hope for your sake that the FPA honors your arrangement."

No waiting. No dragging it out or making the man beg. Nova was quick about killing Ira, although he wasn't friendly about how he delivered the blow.

A snap of Nova's fingers and fire engulfed Ira's body. The witch's shrieks were horrific. Magical fire didn't burn the table or the chair, just the man. Heat filled the room, forcing a few of the others from their chairs. Ghost and I stayed put, waiting for it to be over.

The ear-piercing wails cut off seconds before he slumped over and hit the floor. When Nova waved a hand and the flames went out, the body was a charred, unrecognizable mess. He scowled at the remains before pulling his phone out and firing off a quick message.

Tucking the phone in a back pocket, Nova turned to address our group. "This is what happens to traitors. It doesn't matter what your reason. The Feds know where the house is now. We'll be adding higher security and recruiting more rogues. They'll be set up across town. It's too risky to bring new people here. I'd advise all of you to let this be a lesson you'll never have to learn the hard way if you learn it now.

"One more thing. The Circle of the Veil is more insistent than ever that I get someone on the inside posing as an agent. I'd prefer volunteers. Take a few nights to think about it." Nova dismissed everyone with a wave but pointed a finger at me. "I'd like a word alone with you."

"Good," I quipped, wrinkling my nose at the stench of burnt flesh. "I'd like a word with you as well. Can it be anywhere but here?"

He led me into the adjoined sitting room and slid the pocket door closed behind us. Much smaller than the living room, it was filled with stiff furniture that didn't invite one to sit down. Aside from Corr who sometimes came to read, I never saw anyone in here.

Unable to sit after what I'd just witnessed, I stood in the middle of the room, waiting for Nova to start, even though I had a dozen questions ready to burst out. When I couldn't wait any longer, I blurted, "If the thumb drive was useless, how did you find out about Ira?"

Nova stood just inside the closed door, keeping his distance. Good thing because just the sight of him started a fire beneath my skin. It was the first time we'd been alone since our multi-orgasmic encounter a few nights ago. I'd left his talisman on my dresser, afraid to carry it. Afraid I'd use it for the wrong reasons.

"Once I cornered one of their agents, it didn't take much to get her talking." An evil grin lit up his gorgeous face, taunting the gentle throb of want between my legs. "Under my thrall she told me about Ira. She also told me that they set you and Dalyn up. The bachelor party. They prescreened the girls, knew every face. They knew who you were the second you walked in the door."

The image he painted of himself seducing a Federal agent made me uneasy. And dare I say, jealous? Ick. That was gross and not at all me. The gravity of what he'd learned settled in to leave a bitter taste in my mouth.

"Because of Ira," I concluded, wishing I could have killed the guy myself. The desire to spill blood was almost as strong as the desire Nova's presence ignited. "So seducing the Fed for information, was that sanctioned by The Circle, or were you running rogue with that one?"

We both knew he'd only done it for me. The thumb drive had failed to save me from the chopping block, so Nova had pulled his own strings behind the scenes. I didn't want it to mean as much to me as it did, but standing in that room, gazing into the scarlet depths of his eyes, it meant everything.

This was incredibly not good. I couldn't have feelings for a demon. An incubus demon who'd gotten me hooked on the rush of him and who'd used me as bait. Used me as bait! All the internal screaming at myself made no difference to the first blooms of feelings that sprang up. Curse them.

"It was barely a seduction, more of a flirtation. I did what I had to do to get the information we needed." Nova shrugged. "The Circle wanted to know who the spy was, and I took care of it. Don't worry about them, cherry bomb. I won't let them touch you."

"Don't say that." I waved both hands in the air as the words tumbled out. "You can't make that kind of promise so just… don't. They've got to realize that you're going out of your way to protect me."

With a growl Nova shoved away from the door but stopped himself from coming to me. Fists clenched, his tail lashed about behind him. "Let me deal with that."

"How exactly do you plan to do that, Nova?" My temper rose, and my voice climbed along with it.

I'd just witnessed how The Circle of the Veil dealt with issues. If they saw me as a problem, I was screwed. Even if Nova refused to be the one to take me out, they'd send someone else.

"They got what they wanted for now. They'll leave you alone." With a frustrated huff, Nova stopped holding back and swept forward, wings spread wide as he pulled me into his arms.

I sank into his embrace, finding myself overcome with the need to wrap myself around him. Peering up at my dark star, I dared to ask, "What if I really am the daughter of a demon? Is that why you're so drawn to me?"

Nova frowned and shook his head of dark braids. "Don't do that. Don't try to find a reason for what's happening between us. Nephilim females are rare. Aside from the one that lives here in the city, I know of only two others currently alive in this world. Males, however, not so rare. Records of nephilim births are kept. Each one is assigned a guardian, an angel. Maybe they never knew about you. Though how your birth would be kept a secret, I can't imagine. I'll look into it, ok? We'll find your answers."

While Nova puzzled over the rules and records of nephilim children, I racked my brain for any memory that might help. There was nothing. If my mother had had an affair with a demon, I'd never known about it.

"Most nephilim manifest their first power in early adulthood," Nova continued, kissing the top of my head. That smallest touch sent a jolt all the way to the soles of my feet. "Do you recall any kind of extraordinary ability from before your turn?"

"No, I don't think so. I mean, nothing I can recall at the moment." Holding onto him, staring up into his eyes, I couldn't think about the past. I couldn't think about anything but having Nova inside me again.

Seeing it all over my face, the bastard grinned. "Just so you know, I've been shielding since I arrived. I still am. You're welcome. I warned you how strong the pull would be. If I wasn't shielding, you'd have been naked and begging the second I walked in the door."

"Can I just be naked and begging now?" Being around Nova always made me hot on the inside, but now it was stronger than ever. My inhibitions quickly fled as I contemplated pulling my pants down and bending over for him.

Nova crushed his lips to mine. His kiss was a possession, a bold claim that named me as his. It frightened me how close he'd gotten. With his mere presence able to make me swoon, I should have run screaming in the opposite direction. What Nova did to me was deadly, and I should have been afraid instead of kissing him back like I couldn't get enough.

"I'm sorry I got you into this," he murmured against my lips. Despite his apology he rubbed a hand between my legs.

My gasp was followed by a sly laugh. "Are you kidding? I can quit any time I want. Now if you could just take your pants off, that would be swell. Take mine off too while you're at it."

I pressed lusty kisses to Nova's neck, letting his pulse beat against my tongue. What would his blood taste like? It smelled like power. A deep, dark power that reached into an abyss of black. It called to me, tempting me to taste him.

What the fucking hell had I let this demon do to me?

Before I could give into the wicked temptation, Nova obeyed my command and started taking off his pants. He nodded to the leather easy chair with a wink. "You're on top."

EPILOGUE

Bloodlust crawled through my veins, bringing me alive in the way nothing else did. The way nothing else ever could. Becoming a vampire had been empowering, a liberation from human weakness. I had never experienced the brooding regret I saw among others. It had set me free.

Now I wondered if having demon blood in my veins made it easier to adapt to a life of preying on humans. Or maybe some of us were simply more cut out for murder than others.

Like Ghost. He crept out of the dark behind me, and I whirled to fend him off before he could make a grab for me. We were hunting tonight. A real hunt that would end with a very real kill.

Before Nova had left the house, he'd told me that we were free to hunt as long as nobody saw and we chose someone that would never be missed. No problem there. I had the name of a man who'd started a local dog fighting ring. He and his friends were responsible for dozens of dog thefts in the area.

Now we were on their trail, following two of them as they walked down darkened streets, looking into backyards. Pieces of human crap. Anyone who could be part of such a thing wasn't contributing anything worthwhile to society. Fuck them. They had to go, and we were here to make it happen.

"What do you think, baby girl? We wait until they get to the end of the street there, where that last house is, or we cut down the alley and come around the other side to head them off?" We were a block behind them, so they didn't hear Ghost's raspy inquiry.

Feeling a little devilish, maybe due to the supposed demon blood in my veins, I tapped a finger on my lip and smiled. "You come up from behind and drive them down the alley, where I'll be waiting."

The alley was void of streetlights. Lined with backyards and garages, it was unlikely we'd be seen. Ghost's near black eyes sparked with excitement. He stroked a finger lightly under my chin, like an evil villain with his feline companion.

"Hunting with you is the best fucking foreplay." He gently bit my bottom lip, careful not to pierce the skin. Then he was gone, becoming one with the night as he stalked our prey.

I slipped down the alley and followed it around to where I figured the halfway point would be. By the time Ghost got them this far from the street, most likely running away from him, I'd be set to block their escape.

My blood sang with the rush of the impending kill. This part never got old.

Demon blood. The idea haunted me. I wanted to laugh it off as something that couldn't possibly be true, but part of me just couldn't. And Nova could deny it if he wanted to, but it definitely would explain this thing between us. Why else would an incubus demon who'd likely been with thousands of women be so infatuated with me?

I needed to know more. If there was any chance it could be true, I had to do whatever it took to find out. Of course, if it did turn out that my mother had some secret demon lover, it wouldn't do much other than explain why my father hated me and why my aura was red. It wouldn't change anything about my current circumstances.

Would it?

Hearing voices ahead, I got my head in the game and readied myself. When the two guys rounded a bend in the alley and came into view, every nerve in my body prickled to life. The bloodlust was in control now.

Throwing both hands out before me, I nailed each of them with a psi ball between the ankles. The hit had them tripping and falling in a tangle of quickly moving limbs. Letting them shout and scream wasn't an option. I was on the closest guy in a blink, silencing him with fangs plunged ruthlessly into his carotid.

Ghost emerged from the shadows, savage delight on his face as he went for the other man. Like a striking snake, he too sank fangs into his victim's neck, going for a killing bite. The human never stood a chance against the vampire's lethal attack. Watching Ghost in his element, along with the taste of fresh blood in my mouth, flashed me back to the one and only time we'd hunted together like this. And the way it had ended, me pressed against a building with Ghost thrusting aggressively inside me.

Our eyes met, and I knew he remembered it too. I never could have imagined where it would lead us. Of my three lovers, Ghost was the only one who could relate to my hunger for blood and death. We shared a bloody kiss before disappearing back into the night like we'd never been there at all.

If I wanted to protect the bonds I'd formed, I needed to be prepared for whatever came next. Mastering my blood magic was just the tip of the iceberg. But I'd never achieve control if I didn't master the past trauma that triggered my panic. It was time to face down that fear, no matter what I had to do to accomplish that.

Nova was willing to look into my possible demon parentage. Part of me wanted him to search for answers, while another part felt safer not knowing. It's not like there was anything I could do about it now.

Except there was. I could get really fucking good at being me, no matter what that entailed. So good that The Circle of the Veil would see that I was no rogue. I was every bit as elite as any of them.

Volunteering to get inside the FPA as a mole was a good place to start.

ALSO BY TRINA M. LEE

Each series takes place in the same world.

Alexa O'Brien Huntress

Alexa is a werewolf with a rare power and an attraction to darkness.

If sinfully alluring incubus vampire Arys is anything, it's darkness. Together they create something wild, dangerous and binding. But it doesn't come without a price. Alexa turns to the powerful, deadly men in her life for help uncovering the truth about who and what she really is. Secrets revealed force her to face the ugly truth that not everyone is who she thinks they are. Not even her.

Reverse harem urban fantasy.

Rebel Heart Series

Angel blood runs through her veins.

Half human and half angel, Spike is a rare female nephilim. Like all nephilim, she's caught in the middle of the war between angels and demons. She's doing her best to avoid choosing a side.

Until she meets two mysterious nephilim brothers as different as night and day. Two brothers who need her help. They're about to turn Spike's world upside down.

Romantic urban fantasy.

ABOUT THE AUTHOR

Trina writes urban fantasy that is dark and gritty with a twist of romance and horror but which is ultimately about people in dark places discovering who they are and what they're made of.

A lover of rock music, vampires and muscle cars, Trina is a dreamer who always secretly wanted to be a rockstar. She lives in Alberta, Canada with her bass player husband, ukulele playing daughter and small herd of cats.

Trina loves to hear from readers so don't hesitate to drop her a line on social media or via email. Find her info at trinamlee.net.

Made in the USA
Middletown, DE
11 October 2023

40602999R00099